Mom's Gift

Phil Olson

A SAMUEL FRENCH ACTING EDITION

FOUNDED 1830

SAMUELFRENCH.COM
SAMUELFRENCH-LONDON.CO.UK

FOR PRODUCTION ENQUIRIES

UNITED STATES AND CANADA
Info@SamuelFrench.com
1-866-598-8449

UNITED KINGDOM AND EUROPE
Plays@SamuelFrench-London.co.uk
020-7255-4302

Each title is subject to availability from Samuel French, depending upon country of performance. Please be aware that *MOM'S GIFT* may not be licensed by Samuel French in your territory. Professional and amateur producers should contact the nearest Samuel French office or licensing partner to verify availability.

MUSIC USE NOTE

Licensees are solely responsible for obtaining formal written permission from copyright owners to use copyrighted music in the performance of this play and are strongly cautioned to do so. If no such permission is obtained by the licensee, then the licensee must use only original music that the licensee owns and controls. Licensees are solely responsible and liable for all music clearances and shall indemnify the copyright owners of the play(s) and their licensing agent, Samuel French, against any costs, expenses, losses and liabilities arising from the use of music by licensees. Please contact the appropriate music licensing authority in your territory for the rights to any incidental music.

IMPORTANT BILLING AND CREDIT REQUIREMENTS

If you have obtained performance rights to this title, please refer to your licensing agreement for important billing and credit requirements.

MOM'S GIFT was first produced at the Lonny Chapman Group Repertory Theatre in Los Angeles, California, in December, 2013. The artistic directors were Larry Eisenberg and Chris Winfield, the president was Linda Alznauer, it was directed by Sherry Netherland, the assistant director and sound designer was Steve Shaw, the producer was Laura Coker, the set design and construction was by Chris Winfield, the stage managers/technical directors were Britt Chichester, Mindy B. Schiller and Jennifer Levinson, the lighting design was by Sabrina Beattie, the costume design was by Lynda Pyka, the publicist was Nora Feldman, the marketing was by Ben Goldberg, the program was by Drina Durazo and the cover art was by Doug Haverty. The cast was as follows:

KAT . . . . Gina Yates

BRITTNEY . . . . Trisha Hershberger

MOM . . . . Julia Silverman

DAD . . . . Chris Winfield, Patrick Skelton

TRISH . . . . Lisa McGee-Mann

KEVIN . . . . Cyrus Alexander

MRS. NORQUIST (VOICEOVER) . . . . Laura Coker

The understudies were Paul Cady (Kevin), Joy Darash (Brittney), and Pascale Gigon (Trish).

CHARACTERS

KAT – 30. The older sister. Plain, extremely smart. Acerbic, but likeable, with a sense of humor. Vulnerable and sympathetic. Playfully sarcastic. Not mean spirited.

MOM – 60. Good sense of humor. Deeply caring. Vikings fan.

DAD – 60. A doctor. Nice guy. Reserved. Holds cards close to the vest.

BRITTNEY – 22. The younger sister. Pretty. A Hooters Girl. Peppy, ditzy, sincere, genuine, not sarcastic.

TRISH – 45. Pretty. A nurse. Kind.

KEVIN – 30. Neighbor growing up. Good looking, successful business person, jock in high school.

MRS. NORQUIST *(Voiceover)* – 70's. Neighbor. A little loopy. We never see her. *(Voiceover, can double cast - or if you would like, you can show her)*

PLACE

The living room and front porch of the Swensen family,
in a Minneapolis suburb.

TIME

A warm September day. Dad's birthday.

ACT I – Sunday. Early afternoon.

ACT II – Same day. One minute later.

AUTHOR'S NOTES

References to professional football teams (like the Packers and Vikings) may be replaced with local amateur or professional football teams.

All stage directions were written by the author and are not from a stage manager's book. Please follow those that affect the characters and plot of the story.

FOREWORD

I'm a big fan of quirky, small cast musicals, especially those that have a regional flavor to them, and that is why I write my *Don't Hug Me* musical comedies with my brother, Paul.

Once in awhile, however, I take a break from the *Don't Hug Me* musicals and write something from the heart. I wrote my play, *A Nice Family Gathering*, after my dad passed away. It was a very personal story for me.

Mom's Gift is another departure from my quirky musicals. My mother passed away in 2006 from breast cancer. It was a very emotional time for me. It took me six years to be able to start writing *Mom's Gift* after she died, but I knew I wanted to do something for her, so I started writing the play in 2012.

Although *Mom's Gift* isn't about my real family, the character of Mom in the play has qualities similar to my mother, and some of the lines are things she said. My mother had a wonderful sense of humor until the end. She was faced with tragedy and could still laugh, and I admired that. I don't know if I could do that.

I wanted to capture that spirit in the play by combining a very tragic event with comedy. The comedy in *Mom's Gift* is not broad, but it comes from a very real place, from the tragedy of the underlying story. In *Mom's Gift* we have equal parts comedy and pathos.

In addition to Mom's mission to "get her wings," it's a story about second chances, miscommunication, forgiveness, and moving on when a loved one dies. There are also a few twists in the play that will surprise the audience. I haven't spoken to a single person who has seen the surprise coming at the end.

With *Mom's Gift*, it was important to me that people feel something when they leave the theatre. My hope is that the audience goes thru the same emotions, the same ups and downs that the characters are feeling on stage. After watching every performance during the world premiere and seeing audiences laugh and cry, I feel good about achieving my goal. It's the kind of story my mother would enjoy seeing.

– Phil Olsen

ACT I

(The setting is a living room complete with couch, coffee table, and easy chair. Upstage left is a door to the kitchen. Upstage center is a hallway that leads to the bedrooms (offstage right), and to a den (offstage left). There's a dining table stage left near the kitchen. Downstage left is a small bar with liquor bottles and glasses on it. Downstage right is the front porch of the house, leading to the front door. There's a bench on the porch.)

*(**KAT**, 30, plain, wearing slacks and comfortable shoes, carrying a bottle of Cabernet wine, a computer bag and a purse, walks up to the front porch of the house. As she approaches the porch, she's stopped by **MRS. NORQUIST**, 70's, the neighbor across the street. She can't seem to break away from her. We don't see **MRS. NORQUIST**.)*

MRS. NORQUIST. *(Offstage)* Oh, hey there, is that you, Kathryn?

*(**KAT** turns back and sees **MRS. NORQUIST**.)*

KAT. Oh, hey, there, Mrs. Norquist.

MRS. NORQUIST. *(Offstage)* So, what brings ya back home, then?

KAT. Oh, just a family reunion.

MRS. NORQUIST. *(Offstage)* Oh, I'm sorry.

KAT. Yeah, me too.

MRS. NORQUIST. *(Offstage)* Boy, it's been a long time, huh. Ya look kinda tired, there. Did ya just have a baby?

KAT. *(taken aback)* No. Don't have any babies.

(Tries to break away from her)

MRS. NORQUIST. *(Offstage)* Oh, that's a shame. So are ya married?

KAT. *(Turns back, trying to be nice)* Nope. Not married.

MRS. NORQUIST. *(Offstage)* Oh, that's too bad. Ya have a boyfriend, then?

KAT. *(Still trying to be nice)* Nope. No boyfriend.

(Turns to leave)

MRS. NORQUIST. *(Offstage)* Oh, for cryin' in the bathtub. Not a lot of time before those eggs dry up, there…so is your sister comin' back?

KAT. *(Reluctantly turns back)* Yeah, she'll be here.

MRS. NORQUIST. *(Offstage)* Now <u>she's</u> a looker. Oh, yah. That's okay, though. <u>You</u> got the <u>brains</u>.

KAT. Alrighty –

MRS. NORQUIST. *(Offstage)* I bet <u>she</u> likes men?

KAT. Okay, I'll see you later, there, Mrs. Norquist. Good seeing you.

(Hurries to the front door, opens it and goes in) Hello, anybody home? Hello?…

(She looks around.) Huh. He redecorated… Dad?… Dad?…

*(Imitating **DAD** as she puts the wine on the bar, then sets down her purse and computer bag by the coffee table.)* "Kat's home! Yaay! So happy to see you! Oh, my gosh, you've gotten prettier. I didn't think it was possible. Yaay!"

*(**BRITTNEY**, 22, **KAT**'s sister, enters from the hallway, wearing a bathrobe.)*

BRITTNEY. Oh, hey, Kat, you made it!

KAT. Hey, Britt.

(They hug.)

BRITTNEY. Dad'll be happy to see you.

KAT. I can't imagine why.

BRITTNEY. Well, cause you haven't been around since Mom's funeral.

KAT. Is he here?

BRITTNEY. No, he's at church.

KAT. So, are you still living at home?

BRITTNEY. No, I just came over last night to watch movies with Dad and it got late so I stayed over.

KAT. Hard to cut the umbilical chord, huh?

(She walks over to the bar.)

BRITTNEY. Yeah. So, it's great that you're back!

(Excited) Hey, maybe we can hang out more, you know, watch movies and eat popcorn and have pillow fights. Like we used to.

KAT. Yeah, we never did that.

(Examines the bottles of booze, deciding what to drink.)

BRITTNEY. *(Hopeful)* We can start!

KAT. Are you on crack?

BRITTNEY. *(Excited, rapid fire)* No, I'm just looking forward to spending more time with you. I don't know why we don't. I mean, you just live an hour from me.

KAT. Yeah, I haven't been very social lately. Traveling, not home much, you know.

(Picks up a bottle of Scotch and pours some in a glass.)

BRITTNEY. Right, right, yeah. Anyway, I better get ready. Is that what you're gonna wear?

KAT. *(Turns to BRITT, indignant)* Yes.

BRITTNEY. *(Smiles, sincere)* Okay.

(She exits through the hallway.)

(KAT takes a drink of Scotch.)

MOM. *(Offstage) (From the hallway)* A little early to be drinking, isn't it?

KAT. *(Turning to the hallway)* I'm just having one…

(No one is there.) Brittney?…was that you?

(She looks at the Scotch glass.) Oh, great, I'm hallucinating.

(MOM, 60, steps into the hallway.)

MOM. I'd pace myself. You got a busy day.

KAT. *(Turning to* MOM*)* Brittney, I can make my own decisions–

(Sees who it is) Oh, hey, Mom.

(Realizing, steps back) HOLY CRAP!

MOM. Nice to see you, too.

KAT. *(Looks at the bottle of Scotch)* Never mix Scotch and antihistamines.

MOM. You're not hallucinating.

KAT. *(Puts the bottle down, looks at* MOM*)* It's like a hologram. Okay, turn it off, Brittney. It's not funny.

MOM. I'm not a hologram.

KAT. Whoa, it's interactive. How cool is that? *(*MOM *steps forward into the room)* Whoa, it's moving!

MOM. Actually, I'm a ghost.

KAT. Nope. No, you're not. No such thing.

(Looking around) Okay, you got me. I've been punked. Come on out.

MOM. I'm not a bad ghost. I mean, it's not like I'm here to haunt you.

KAT. *(Looking around for the projector)* Where are you coming from? I mean the technology is really good.

MOM. There's no technology. It's just me. I'm a ghost.

KAT. Oh, okay.

(Whispering) Why are you here?

MOM. What are you doing?

KAT. Ghost whispering.

MOM. Alright, just so we can move this thing along, why don't we do this, just pretend, for the sake of argument, that I'm a figment of your imagination. I'm in your head. You know, you haven't gotten over my death, you're distraught, you wish I were still alive, you're seeing things, yada yada yada.

KAT. I never should have done those mushrooms in college.

MOM. You did mushrooms in college!?

KAT. Really? I'm gonna argue about college mushrooms with Ghost Mom?

MOM. Okay, let's do this. I'm not going away, okay. So you have a choice, fight it or go along with it. What's it gonna be?

KAT. *(Holding up her index finger)* One minute.

(She turns away from **MOM**.*)* I am totally losing it.

(Takes a deep breath) Be strong. If this is how I'm gonna handle the stress of today, just go with it.

(Composes herself, turns to **MOM***)* Okay, fine. You're in my head. A figment.

(Realizing) An imaginary friend! Like when I was a kid! You know what, this could make the day go faster. I'm talking to myself and I'm crazy. Super! Okay, and you're here because…?

MOM. They sent me back. Unfinished business, your spirit can't rest until you come to peace. You know the program.

KAT. No, I seriously do not know the program.

MOM. I've been floating around in limbo for 11 months and I can't move on until I resolve something.

KAT. We're Lutheran. We don't have limbo.

MOM. Then what do we have?

KAT. Pot lucks.

MOM. Oh, for Pete's sake. Look, all I know is it's kind of like Clarence in "It's a Wonderful Life." You know, "when a bell rings, an angel gets it's wings."

KAT. Isn't that the movie about the irresponsible bankers who lose their customers money, drive drunk, have their debts paid off by local citizens and suffer no consequences for their carelessness.

MOM. Yeah, that's it.

KAT. I never saw it.

MOM. Okay, I'll get to the point. I need you to help me.

KAT. You want my help? Isn't that like cheating? So, now you can cheat to get into Heaven?

(Realizing) Maybe you're not going to Heaven.

MOM. Funny.

KAT. By the way, is there a Heaven? I never really bought into that.

MOM. For some people. You, I wouldn't hold my breath.

KAT. Whoa! A zinger! Wait, you're in my mind. That's coming from me. This is confusing.

MOM. They said I could get help from you.

KAT. They who?

(MOM points up) Oh, up there. Really? Did they name me specifically? Because I don't sense that I'm on their radar.

MOM. Are you gonna help me or not?

KAT. Okay, so if I help you, do you and these voices in my head go away?

MOM. Since we're going with that narrative, yes.

KAT. Okay, fine. What do you want me to do?

MOM. I need you to help me complete a mission.

KAT. Can you be more specific?

MOM. I have to either heal a wound, right a wrong, help someone in need, or fix a relationship.

KAT. Well that narrows it down.

MOM. They don't tell you the mission. We have to discover what it is.

KAT. "We?!"

MOM. And it has to happen today, while you're here.

KAT. And if it doesn't?

MOM. *(Overly dramatic)* I go back into the system, and trust me, you don't wanna be stuck in the system. Floating around in Lutheran limbo for eternity, never to make it thru the pearly gates. Who knows where I'll end up. Maybe they'll send me down there…

(Gestures and looks down) Or worse…to New Jersey.

KAT. You been working on that?

MOM. Yeah, you like it?

KAT. Yeah, not bad… Look, I don't even wanna be here let alone be dragged into your angel scavenger hunt.

MOM. If you don't wanna be here, then why are you here?

KAT. My therapist told me I had to come here as an exercise in anger management.

MOM. You go to a therapist?

KAT. I went one time!… Okay, six times.

MOM. Why?

KAT. Because I, sort of…shoved a cop.

MOM. I'm sorry, what?

KAT. Okay, after your funeral–that is so weird to say. After your funeral I got in a big argument with Dad, drove off and got a speeding ticket–you don't know this?!

MOM. They don't let you see everything until you *(Looks up)* get your wings!

KAT. Fine. A cop pulled me over for speeding, I was angry and I told him he had a tiny night stick. He thought I was drunk, made me walk the line, got into my personal space, and I… kind of shoved him.

MOM. You were always a little high tempered.

KAT. I am not high tempered!

MOM. You seem a little bound up. Are you regular?

KAT. Oh, my gosh! It was just a little shove! Come on, the guy was huge. It wasn't a big deal!!
(Catching herself, taking a deep breath, closes her eyes, does a zen-like movement with her hands) Control your anger. Don't let it control you.

MOM. At the risk of setting you off again, isn't it a crime to shove a cop?

KAT. Well, because of the circumstance, distraught and whatever, they said they wouldn't charge me if I went to see a therapist.

MOM. Well, that was nice of 'em.

KAT. Not really. The therapist ordered me to go to Dad's birthday party.

MOM. You were ordered by the court to spend time with your dad?

KAT. I know. Cruel and unusual punishment.

MOM. Wow. Daughter of the year.

KAT. Thank you, "figment!"

MOM. What if you don't go thru with it? I mean, walk out and leave right now.

KAT. I'll be charged with felony assault, lose my job and go to jail.

MOM. How will the court know you came here?

KAT. I have to have a witness sign a contract. I can't believe it. I've been sentenced to spend Dad's birthday with him. And what's worse, I can't yell at him. Not even once. It's in the contract.

MOM. *(Realizing)* Okay, that's it. I know what my mission is. Help you make peace with your dad.

KAT. How about if you just compliment me for an hour?

MOM. Why would I do that? No, it's gotta be bigger. I need to help you resolve your differences with Dad.

KAT. Yeah, I don't know if I can work with you on that. I mean, I'm just here to serve my sentence, pick up some of my things and tell him I'm leaving for a few years. Kind of a last supper.

MOM. Wait, you're leaving for a few years? Where are you going?

(**DAD**, *60 enters the front door.*)

DAD. I'm home.

MOM. Hi, honey.

(**DAD** *walks past* **MOM**, *setting his keys on the table.*)

KAT. *(to Mom)* He can't see you?

MOM. I'm in your head, remember?

(**DAD** *looks over to* **KAT**.)

DAD. Hey, Kat, I'm so glad you could be here.

KAT. Really?

DAD. Yes, of course.

*(***DAD*** *goes to hug ***KAT**. *It's the most awkward, arm's length, pat on the shoulders hug, imaginable.)*

KAT. *(As she continues to pat his shoulders, arms length.)* Yeah, well, you know, it's your birthday.

MOM. Worst hug ever!

KAT. *(To ***MOM***)* HUSH!

DAD. I'm sorry, what?

*(***BRITTNEY*** *enters from the hallway.)*

KAT. *(Covering)* Hush…

*(To ***MOM***, spoken)* little mamma, don't say a word–

*(Motions to ***MOM*** to zip her lips)*

BRITTNEY. *(Singing)*

PAPA'S GONNA BUY YOU A MOCKINGBIRD. AND IF THAT–

KAT. *(Cutting her off)* Okay, thank you. Very good. You know the words. Great.

BRITTNEY. *(To ***DAD***)* How was church?

DAD. Good. Kat, you should go with me sometime.

KAT. Yeah, I'm not really a church person. I'm more of a brunch person.

BRITTNEY. You used to go to church. What happened?

KAT. *(Short)* Britt, it's Sunday. This is no time to talk about religion.

DAD. Can I get you something? A can of pop, or–

KAT. How about a Scotch? A double. Wait, do you have Jagermeister? No, just Scotch, that's fine.

*(***DAD*** *goes to the bar to make the drink.)*

DAD. I didn't know you were a drinker.

KAT. I just started.

MOM. Easy, now. I need you alert for this.

KAT. *(Shoots ***MOM*** a look)* You re-decorated.

DAD. Yeah, I changed a few things.

KAT. A lot of things.

DAD. So, what have you been up to? I haven't seen you since the funeral.

BRITTNEY. That was eleven months ago.

KAT. I know. I just… I've been really busy at work.

BRITTNEY. What do you do again?

KAT. I'm an environmental aquatic engineer.

BRITTNEY. Oh, yeah… I don't know what that is.

KAT. I make water.

BRITTNEY. Oh, yeah. Like Jesus.

KAT. Yup. Just like Jesus.

MOM. Brittney hasn't changed.

DAD. So, what project are you working on now?

KAT. Right now I'm designing engines that purify water using reverse osmosis. They take any kind of polluted or contaminated water and make it potable. *(pron. poh-tuh-buhl)*

(*To* **BRITTNEY**, *condescending*) That means you can drink it.

DAD. So, you help supply water to…?

KAT. To third world countries.

BRITTNEY. Whoa, whoa, whoa. I thought we only had <u>one</u> world.

MOM. Wow.

KAT. You know, if we could harness the water between your ears, we could power a city.

BRITTNEY. Why don't we?

KAT. *(Changing the subject)* So, what are you doing these days, Britt?

BRITTNEY. Oh, I'm a waitress.

KAT. What restaurant?

BRITTNEY. Hooters.

KAT. You're a Hooters Girl?

BRITTNEY. Uh huh.

KAT. *(Sarcastic)* I am so proud of you.

BRITTNEY. Really?!–

KAT. No.

MOM. Don't do it.

KAT. Are you still going to junior college?

BRITTNEY. No, too much memorizing. I'm not really a memory person.

KAT. You're more of a <u>mammary</u> person.

MOM. Easy.

DAD. She actually makes pretty good money.

KAT. Enough to pay your own rent?

BRITTNEY. Almost.

KAT. *(To **DAD**)* So, you're still helping her out?

DAD. She's my angel.

KAT. How's that drink coming?
(He hands it to her) Thank you.

DAD. I'm really glad you're here.

KAT. Hey, I had to come.
(They hear a knock at the door.)

DAD. Oh, that must be Trish.

KAT. Trish?
*(**DAD** opens the door. We see **TRISH**, an attractive 45 year old woman, carrying two grocery bags, a purse and a tote bag over her shoulder, wearing a conservative top with a high neckline.)*

DAD. Hi, come on in.

TRISH. *(She enters.)* Happy birthday.

DAD. Thanks.

MOM. Oh, my gosh, it's Trish. She looks great.
*(**DAD** takes the groceries from **TRISH**. **TRISH** is a little nervous, breathing heavy. **DAD** notices.)*

DAD. You look a little flush. Are you okay?

TRISH. Yeah, just a little winded.

DAD. Trish, this is my daughter, Kat, and you remember Brittney. (**DAD** *sets the groceries on the dining table.*)

TRISH. Hi.

BRITTNEY. Nice to see you again.

TRISH. Thank you. It's nice to see you, too.

MOM. Be nice to her.

KAT. You took care of Mom after the accident, right?

TRISH. Yes, I was with her for the last few weeks.

MOM. She was wonderful. I could not have died without her.

KAT. Were you her nurse?

TRISH. Actually, I kept your mother company, made her meals, you know, things like that.

KAT. Like a care giver.

TRISH. Exactly. We actually became friends.

KAT. Uh huh…

(*Suspicious*) and now you're back.

TRISH. Your dad invited me. I thought that was really nice.

DAD. I had an ulterior motive. She offered to make dinner.

MOM. She's a good cook.

BRITTNEY. Oh, I love to cook. Can I help?

TRISH. Absolutely.

DAD. (*To* **TRISH**) Can I get you a drink or something?

TRISH. How about a Diet Coke?

DAD. Coming right up.

TRISH. I'll just put these in the kitchen.

(*She grabs the groceries and heads for the kitchen.* **BRITT** *follows her.* **DAD** *goes to the bar to pour the Diet Coke.*)

KAT. The kitchen is right in…oh, of course, you know where it is.

(**TRISH** *and* **BRITT** *go in the kitchen. To* **DAD**, *awkward.*) So… Trish is here.

MOM. She's very nice.

DAD. She was a big help with your mom.

KAT. I don't remember, was she at Mom's funeral?

DAD. Oh, no, she wasn't there. She had to attend a family matter in Ohio.

KAT. Uh huh.

DAD. We re-connected a few months after the funeral.

KAT. "Re-connected?"

DAD. Well, I mean, we saw each other again.

MOM. It's innocent.

KAT. Uh huh... So, where are the photos of Mom?

DAD. The what?

KAT. You used to have family photos with Mom on the wall. What did you do with 'em?

DAD. Oh, I, ah... I took them down.

KAT. Why did you do that?

MOM. This isn't resolving!

BRITTNEY. *(Coming out of the kitchen)* Anyone wanna try a mini-muffin top? *(Holding out a tray)* I made 'em myself.

KAT. No, thanks.

DAD. I'll try one.

   (Takes one, takes a bite)

BRITTNEY. Mom used to make 'em.

MOM. I'd like one! Wait,

   (Looks up) can I eat?

BRITTNEY. *(To* **DAD***)* What do you think?

DAD. Wow, these are really good.

BRITTNEY. I used her recipe.

DAD. Your mom was a great cook.

MOM. *(Humble)* Oh, you shouldn't.

   (Then) Okay, you should.

DAD. You should enter 'em in a baking contest. Pillsbury has one. You might win something.

BRITTNEY. Yeah, that's something I wanted to talk to you about.

KAT. Why did you take Mom's photos down?

MOM. Keep it together!

KAT. *(To* **MOM***)* You're right. Breathe.
(Takes a deep breath, closes her eyes, does a zen-like movement with her hands.) Anger is the prison of the soul.

BRITTNEY. What are you doing?

KAT. Breathing exercise. It helps me to–

MOM. To not be such a butt head.

KAT. *(Looks at* **MOM***)* To relax.

DAD. You feeling stress? Is it work?

KAT. No, it's nothing. I'll be fine.

*(**TRISH** comes out of the kitchen.)*

TRISH. So, Kat, I hear you're an engineer.

KAT. Yes, I am. Did Dad tell you that?

TRISH. Your mom did.

*(**DAD** hands **TRISH** a glass of Diet Coke. Trish mouths, "thank you.")*

KAT. Right.

TRISH. A degree in mathematics from Dartmouth, an engineering degree from M.I.T. That's really impressive.

KAT. Thanks.

BRITTNEY. Kat makes water. Like Jesus.

KAT. Technically, Jesus didn't make water. He made wine <u>from</u> water. He walked on water, but he didn't make water. That is, if you believe any of that stuff. Dad, why did you take down the photos of Mom?

MOM. You have no filter.

DAD. Honey, it's been difficult since your mom… *(He can't say it.)*

KAT. Since she died. From a car accident. You were driving, remember?

MOM. Stop it! Right now! You need to get past this.

DAD. *(Sadly)* Yes. Of course I remember.

BRITTNEY. *(To* **KAT***)* Why are you being like this?

(**KAT** *takes a deep breath.*) It's stress. She needs drugs. Dad, do you have any Xanax? Wait, I might have one.

KAT. I don't need drugs, just alcohol.

(She takes a sip of her drink.)

DAD. *(To* **BRITTNEY***)* Why would you have Xanax?

BRITTNEY. *(Busted)* What happened? Did I say that? Tourettes!

TRISH. Sometimes it takes a long time to heal after a loved one dies.

KAT. I'll be fine. I'm just going thru a thing.

TRISH. I'm very sorry about your mother. She was a wonderful person.

MOM. I really like her.

TRISH. I mean, the short time that I spent with her…

(Emotional) she really changed my life.

MOM. I really, really like her.

BRITTNEY. *(Holds up the plate)* Who wants a muffin top?

TRISH. Oh, I'd like one.

(Takes one, takes a bite)

KAT. No, thanks.

MOM. *(To* **KAT***)* Maybe if <u>you</u> eat one, <u>I'll</u> taste it.

BRITTNEY. What do you think?

TRISH. Wow, these are good.

BRITTNEY. Thanks.

(Looks at her cell phone) Oh, I just got a text from my boyfriend.

DAD. I didn't know you had a boyfriend.

BRITTNEY. Just for a couple months.

MOM. Good for you.

DAD. What's his name?

BRITTNEY. Manson.

KAT. Manson? As in Charles Manson?

BRITTNEY. Oh, no. My Manson hasn't been in prison for years.

DAD. You're kidding, right? *(To* **KAT***)* Is she kidding?

MOM. Let's hope.

BRITTNEY. I didn't wanna say anything until it got more serious.

DAD. It's serious?!

BRITTNEY. Well, sort of.

KAT. What does he do now? I mean, you know, since prison.

BRITTNEY. He's an engineer. Like you.

MOM. Well, that's good.

KAT. What kind of an engineer?

BRITTNEY. A custodial engineer.

KAT. A janitor?

MOM. Lovely.

BRITTNEY. Yeah, he's been working for 14 years at Hubert Humphrey Elementary School.

KAT. How old is he?

BRITTNEY. He's 37.

MOM. He's what?

DAD. He's 15 years older than you are?

BRITTNEY. But he thinks so young. I mean, it's like we're the same age.

DAD. Where did you meet him?

BRITTNEY. Hooters.

MOM. *(Looking up)* Just take me now.

TRISH. I think I'll get the appetizers ready.

(She heads for the kitchen.)

DAD. I think I'll help you.

(He follows her.)

BRITTNEY. I like Trish.

MOM. So do I.

KAT. You're dating a 37 year old ex-con?

BRITTNEY. But he's so young. I mean, he rides a skateboard.

MOM. *(Looking up)* Is this part of the test?

BRITTNEY. And he has, like, nine tattoos.

MOM. *(Groans)* Ohhh!

KAT. Are you sure you weren't adopted?

BRITTNEY. Maybe <u>you</u> were adopted.

MOM. No one was adopted…

    (Disappointed) Dammit.

KAT. You almost gave Dad a heart attack. That was awesome.

BRITTNEY. Well, I didn't mean to.

MOM. Yes, you did.

KAT. *(To MOM)* She's just a–

BRITTNEY. A what?

MOM. You don't know her.

BRITTNEY. I'm just a what?

KAT. *(Covering)* You're just a…daddy's little girl.

BRITTNEY. Oh, yeah. Does that bother you?

KAT. *(Ignoring the question)* Why did Dad take Mom's pictures down?

BRITTNEY. It's been really difficult for Dad. He's trying to forget.

KAT. Forget Mom?

BRITTNEY. You know what I'm talking about.

KAT. What's the deal with Trish?

BRITTNEY. What do you mean?

KAT. Has he been seeing her?

MOM. They're just friends.

BRITTNEY. I think they go out maybe once or twice a week.

KAT. That's dating.

    *(**DAD** comes out of the kitchen with a bowl of chips and sets it on the dining table.)*

DAD. It's good to see you, Kat. I know we didn't end things well after the funeral.

KAT. Yeah, well, funerals will do that.

MOM. Here's your chance to make up with him.

DAD. I know you were upset at my decision.

KAT. You took Mom off life support. You didn't even discuss it with me.

DAD. Well, you were in India.

MOM. He's a doctor. He knew what he was doing.

KAT. You told me she was getting better.

DAD. I thought she was.

KAT. You couldn't wait until I got back?

MOM. This is making up?

DAD. It was tearing me up to see her like that.

KAT. I didn't even get to say goodbye.

DAD. Well, I'm sorry.

> (**TRISH** *comes out of the kitchen with a plate of appetizers.*)

KAT. Just like you're sorry for getting in the car accident?

MOM. Not helping the mission.

DAD. It was a hit and run. They ran a red light. Drunk driver, they think. You know that.

> (*Upon hearing that,* **TRISH** *puts the appetizers on the table, and does an about face, going back into the kitchen.* **KAT** *notices.*)

You know, I really hope that some day you can forgive me. (**KAT** *doesn't respond*) Look, I know you're busy, but it would be real nice if maybe we could spend a little more time together.

KAT. I wish you would have said that twenty years ago.

DAD. Is that what this is about? Not spending enough time with you when you were kids?

MOM. He was busy providing for you.

BRITTNEY. (*Singing Harry Chapin's "Cat's in the Cradle"*)*
THE CAT'S IN THE CRADLE AND THE SILVER SPOON...

> (*Everyone looks at her. She stops.*)

---

*Please see Music Use Note on page 3

KAT. You know what, it's okay. It doesn't matter.

DAD. Yes, it does.

KAT. No, it doesn't. I'm leaving in a couple weeks. I'll be gone for about a year. Maybe two.

DAD. You're what?

MOM. Where are you going?

KAT. We're installing several engines that will provide water to towns in Somalia. Oh, that reminds me. I need to send an email.

(**KAT** *goes to her computer bag by the coffee table, takes out her computer, opens it up, and goes into her email account.*)

DAD. You're going to Somalia?!

KAT. Yes.

DAD. Honey, Somalia is really dangerous.

KAT. It's gotten better.

BRITTNEY. Isn't that where all the pirates are?

DAD. The Marines don't even go to Somalia. Remember "Black Hawk Down?" The Marines said, "We're outta here!" The Marines!

(**KAT** *types in her email.*)

BRITTNEY. Dad, if you're worried about the ransom, they have kidnapping insurance.

MOM. Oh, my gosh.

DAD. Not helping.

BRITTNEY. But it's, like, really expensive cause there are, like, sooo many kidnappings.

DAD. Isn't that the responsibility of the company?

KAT. Are you trying to get out of paying my ransom?

DAD. No, I'll pay your ransom. Look, no one's getting kidnapped, okay, but the fact that we're even talking about it worries me, honey.

KAT. Don't worry, I don't spend the whole time in Somalia.

DAD. Okay.

KAT. I also go to Ghana, The Congo, Rwanda and Libya.

DAD. *(Sarcastic)* Well, <u>that's</u> a relief.

KAT. They need water.

DAD. Can't you just go somewhere like Fiji?

KAT. Fiji already has water.

DAD. Honey, why are you doing this?

KAT. Because they need me.

DAD. Can't they send someone else? I mean, you're always trying to save the world, helping others, which is admirable, but if you don't do something for yourself, you won't have anything to offer anyone else.

BRITTNEY. It takes a village!…

(*A beat, looks around*) I read that on a Snapple cap.

MOM. *(Laughs. KAT shoots her a look.)* It's funny.

KAT. Dad, I enjoy doing things for other people.

MOM. Hah!

(*KAT rolls her eyes.*)

(*TRISH comes out of the kitchen with a "Happy Birthday" centerpiece. KAT sees TRISH.*)

DAD. What about your family and friends?

KAT. I'll email you. And I'm not sure where my family is, anyway. They aren't on the wall.

(*Testing TRISH*) I guess because a drunk driver took one of them. (*She looks at TRISH to see her reaction.*)

(*Upon hearing that, TRISH sets the "Happy Birthday" centerpiece on the dining table, then goes back in the kitchen. KAT watches TRISH leave.*)

DAD. You think I don't feel guilty about that?

KAT. I don't know.

DAD. Are you doing this to punish me?

(*KAT doesn't respond.*)

Congratulations. It worked.

BRITTNEY. I'm gonna see if Trish needs any help.

(She goes into the kitchen.)

KAT. Look, it's just part of my healing, you know, to get it all out.

DAD. Honey, I'm worried about you. I really am.

MOM. So am I.

KAT. Why? I'm fine.

DAD. Have you considered seeing a therapist?

MOM. *(Leaning into* **KAT***)* Tell him.

KAT. Why would you say that? Look, it's just that… I've been thinking a lot about Mom lately. It's like she's right here, just…in my face. All the time.
(Moving her hand like a talking sock puppet) Wah, wah, wah, wah, wah.

MOM. I love you, too.

DAD. Is there anything I can do? Maybe prescribe something?

KAT. Is that your answer? Drugs and therapy?

DAD. I'm just trying to help.

KAT. Then help me understand why you removed every trace of Mom from the house.

DAD. Because I'm moving on with my life. And you should too. *(He goes into the den)*

KAT. That was harsh.

MOM. I wouldn't call this resolving your differences with Dad.

KAT. How do you even know that's your mission?

MOM. It's obvious he wants to spend more time with you.

KAT. Yeah, why now?

MOM. I don't know, I guess because, duh, life is short. And besides, aren't you supposed to get along with him? I mean, that's what the contract says, right?

KAT. Yeah, you're right. I just need to make it thru today. *(Takes a deep breath, closes her eyes, does a zen-like movement with her hands)* Anger is one letter short of danger.

MOM. Your dad has a point, you know.

KAT. You're siding with Dad? The guy who's "moving on" with his life?

MOM. That's the problem. He's <u>not</u> moving on.

KAT. Oh, you sound like my therapist.

MOM. What do you do for fun?

KAT. When I'm not watching Animal Planet, I go on the Papa John's website and build my dream pizza.

MOM. Don't you wanna settle down some day and get married?

KAT. Yeah, well, I thought I might for awhile. But, you know what I discovered? It's not really up to me.

MOM. Why not?

KAT. Remember when you called me "Princess" when I was little?

MOM. Yeah.

KAT. Yeah, well, later in life no one else was on board with that.

MOM. You should get one of those self esteem workbooks.

KAT. I have six of them.

MOM. I think you have a lot going for yourself and there are a lot of guys that would love to be with you.
(*Realizing*) Maybe <u>that's</u> my mission. To find you a guy.

KAT. Yeah, then what? Spend the rest of my life with the same person?

MOM. When you find the right guy, like I did with your dad, you never want to let him go.

KAT. You don't have any regrets about marrying Dad?

MOM. No. Not at all. He was kind and funny and great in bed.

KAT. Mom!

(**DAD** *comes out of the den.*)

MOM. He was the greatest partner anyone could ever have.

DAD. Who are you talking to?

KAT. Oh, I'm just, umm…practicing a speech.

DAD. Have you looked at any of your mom's things?

KAT. No, why?

DAD. *(Calling to the kitchen)* Hey, Brittney!

 *(To **KAT**)* She's got a whole bunch of stuff in the back–

 *(**BRITTNEY** comes out of the kitchen, followed by **TRISH**.)*

BRITTNEY. What's up?

DAD. Your mom has some things she wanted you girls to have, clothes and jewelry and stuff. You wanna take a look at it?

BRITTNEY. Yes!

KAT. Yeah, in a little bit.

MOM. Why wait?

DAD. I'll show you where it is.

 (Starts for the back room)

MOM. *(To **KAT**)* There's something in there you need to see.

DAD. *(Turning back, to **TRISH**)* Oh, can I get you anything?

TRISH. No, I'm fine. Go ahead.

DAD. Game is on in the den, Vikings, Packers, if you wanna check it out.

TRISH. And you're out here?

DAD. I'm recording it.

TRISH. Oh, by the way, how's your fantasy team doing?

DAD. Really? You had to bring that up? On my birthday?

TRISH. Oh, I'm sorry, did I strike a nerve?

DAD. *(To **KAT**)* Her fantasy team is beating mine.

 *(To **TRISH**)* Thanks. Thank you. Oh, hey, how's your golf game?

TRISH. Oh, that is not fair bringing up my golf skills.

DAD. *(Playful)* Oh, I'm sorry, those aren't skills.

BRITTNEY. Oh, it's a smackdown.

DAD. *(Smiling)* It's my birthday.

TRISH. *(Playful)* Yes, and you've had five dozen of 'em.

BRITTNEY. Whoa!

DAD. *(To* **TRISH,** *smiling)*

Alright, serve it on–

(Quickly to **BRITT***)*

What's the saying?–

BRITTNEY. Nope! Nope! You're too old, Dad. Let's go.

*(***BRITT** *leads* **DAD** *thru the hallway into the back room, stage right.)*

MOM. Your dad and Trish seem to get along.

*(***KAT** *and* **TRISH** *look at each other. It's awkward.)*

KAT. *(To* **TRISH***)* So, it's nice that you could be here for Dad's birthday.

TRISH. Oh, well, he's been a good friend.

MOM. See, they're just friends.

KAT. Yeah, it's good to have friends. I just, sometimes find it hard to have guy friends.

MOM. Oh, for good grief.

KAT. I mean, there's always something more going on when there's a guy involved.

TRISH. Yeah, sometimes their motives are a little confusing.

KAT. Tell me about it.

TRISH. Why is it so hard to find men who are sensitive, caring and good looking?

KAT. I have no idea.

TRISH. Because those men already have boyfriends. *(She smiles.* **KAT** *laughs)*

MOM. *(Laughs, to* **KAT***)* That was good.

TRISH. You know, I bet you have a lot of guy friends. I mean, being an engineer and all isn't exactly a field you see a lot of women in. And you have so much going for yourself, I bet a lot of guys want to be friends with you.

KAT. *(Flattered)* Oh, well, I don't know.

TRISH. Your mother talked about you a lot.

KAT. She did?

TRISH. Yeah, she was really inspired by your work.

KAT. *(Looking at* **MOM***)* Really?

MOM. That surprises you?

TRISH. She told me that six thousand children die every day from a lack of clean water.

KAT. Yeah, it's a real problem.

TRISH. It is. And you're helping to solve it, and she really admired you for that. For the impact you had on people's lives.

KAT. *(To* **MOM***)* Oh, well, I think she had a pretty big impact, too.

TRISH. Yeah. Hey, I'm gonna go cheer for the Vikings. You wanna come watch the game?

KAT. No, that's okay. Go ahead.

*(***TRISH** *exits to the den.)*

MOM. She's like Mother Teresa with a sense of humor.

KAT. *(Skeptical)* She's good. She's very good.

MOM. She's a nice person.

KAT. There's something else going on there.

MOM. Yeah. She's a Vikings fan.

BRITTNEY. *(Entering. To* **KAT***)* Hey, check out the photo on Mom's driver's license. *(Hands* **KAT MOM***'s driver's license)*

KAT. *(Re; the horrible photo, laughing)* Oh, my gosh!

MOM. They didn't say "cheese!"

BRITTNEY. Come look at her stuff.

KAT. Yeah, I'll be there in a little bit.

MOM. Look at it now.

KAT. I'm just having a little trouble with the idea of pillaging thru Mom's things.

BRITTNEY. *(Smiles)* Okay.

(She disappears into the hallway)

MOM. *(To* **BRITTNEY***, as she leaves)* Look in the brown bag, back of the closet.

BRITTNEY. *(Coming back, to* **KAT***)* You say something?

KAT. No.

BRITTNEY. Huh.

(She disappears into the hallway)

KAT. *(Reading* **MOM***'s license)* "Margaret Ann Swensen. Five seven, green eyes, donor, weight, a hundred and nine!?" Hah! So, now you're writing fiction?

MOM. I weighed a hundred and nine once! Listen, you better get in there before Brittney takes everything.

KAT. She's like a vulture picking at a carcass.

MOM. So, now I'm a carcass?

KAT. No, but you're becoming a pain in the carcass.

MOM. *(Re: their banter)* Oh, I miss this… And you're still jealous of Brittney.

KAT. Jealous? Brittney's the reason they put instructions on shampoo bottles.

MOM. You can't judge a book by its cover.

KAT. Brittney's not a book. She's a pamphlet.

MOM. You should get to know her. You never did growing up.

KAT. She was on training wheels when I was learning to drive.

MOM. It's not too late. Now, are you gonna look at my things, or what? There's something in there you need to see.

*(***KAT** *looks out the window. Up the walk comes* **KEVIN***, 30, handsome, wearing a sport coat.)*

KAT. Fine, fine, I'll go…is that Kevin Reese?

MOM. *(Looking)* Yeah. Wow, he's more handsome than I remembered.

KAT. He's coming up to our door. What's he doing here?

MRS. NORQUIST. *(Offstage)* Is that you, Kevin?

KEVIN. *(Turning back)* Oh, hey there, Mrs. Norquist.

MRS. NORQUIST. *(Offstage)* I didn't recognize ya with all those muscles.

KEVIN. Oh, well, I grew up.

MRS. NORQUIST. *(Offstage)* Ya look like a Chippendale Dancer.

KEVIN. *(Taken aback)* So, how's <u>Mr.</u> Norquist?

MRS. NORQUIST. *(Offstage)* He's dead.

KEVIN. He's mowing the lawn.

MRS. NORQUIST. *(Offstage)* That's a zombie.

KEVIN. Alrighty.

MRS. NORQUIST. *(Offstage)* Come here for a second. I can't see ya. I got cataracts.

KEVIN. *(Hesitant)* Oh, umm, I'm actually–

MRS. NORQUIST. *(Offstage)* Oh, come on! I got some candy!

KEVIN. *(To himself)* Oh, boy.

(He takes a few steps back toward **MRS. NORQUIST***)*

MOM. Make yourself look nice. Are you gonna wear that?

KAT. We'll I'm not gonna change.

MOM. I'm just saying, would it kill you to wear a dress?

KAT. I thought you said you weren't gonna haunt me.

MOM. What? You've had a crush on him since elementary school.

KAT. I have not. I hated him. He made my life a living hell.

MOM. You had a telescope in your bedroom so you could spy on him.

KAT. It was for school!

MOM. Really? What class? Voyeurism 101?

MRS. NORQUIST. *(Offstage)* So, are ya married?

KEVIN. Nope, not married.

MRS. NORQUIST. *(Offstage)* Oh, you should ask out Brittney. The other one hates men.

KEVIN. Okay.

MRS. NORQUIST. *(Offstage)* If I were younger, I'd be on you like Cheese Whiz on a cracker.

KEVIN. Okay, Mrs. Norquist–

MRS. NORQUIST. *(Offstage)* I'm the Cheese Whiz and you're the cracker.

KEVIN. Alrighty–

MRS. NORQUIST. *(Offstage)* Saltine. Cause ya look salty.

KEVIN. Okay, good seeing you–

MRS. NORQUIST. *(Offstage)* You wanna see my tattoos?

KEVIN. *(Shielding his eyes)*
No! No!–

(Takes a peek. She flashes her tattoos. Grossed out)
Ohh!

(He gags, turns and hurries toward the door.)

MOM. Here he comes. Last chance to make yourself look presentable.

(He knocks on the door. **KAT** *doesn't move.)*

KAT. He's knocking! What do I do?

MOM. Go and bleach your mustache.

KAT. Really?!

MOM. You have Al Queda facial hair.

KAT. Mom!

MOM. I'd hate to see what's going on…
(Motions to "below **KAT***'s belt")* down there.

KAT. Oh, my gosh!

(He knocks again.)

MOM. Answer the door. But fix your hair first.
(Re: her hair) Seriously, it's like a rat's nest.

KAT. No! Maybe he'll think no one is home and go away.

MOM. He can see you! Oh, for goodness sake, answer the door. Stand up straight. And smile. You'll be more attractive.

KAT. Mom!

(Takes a deep breath)

(**KAT** *opens the door and smiles.*)

KEVIN. Hey, Kat, long time no see.

KAT. Yeah…

(After a few awkward beats) And you are…?

KEVIN. Kevin Reese. We grew up together. Neighbors. Remember?

(Points to his parent's house.) Right over there?

(**DAD** *comes out of the hallway.*)

KAT. Oh, yeah, right.

(An awkward pause) Okay, good catching up.

(She starts to close the door.)

DAD. Is that Kevin?

KEVIN. Hey, Dr. Swensen. Happy birthday.

DAD. Oh, come on, call me Jack, would ya?

KEVIN. Yeah, sorry, it's hard to get used to.

DAD. Come on in. Kat, you remember Kevin.

KAT. Yeah, I guess we grew up together.

KEVIN. I'm really sorry to hear about your mom.

KAT. Thanks.

KEVIN. She was a wonderful person.

MOM. Oh, how sweet.

DAD. Yes, she was. Thanks.

(**BRITT** *enters from the hallway wearing one of* **MOM**'s *dresses.*)

BRITTNEY. Hey, Kevin, good to see you.

(She hugs him. **KAT** *notices the familiarity.)*

KEVIN. Hey Britt.

BRITTNEY. *(Flirtatious)* You look good.

KEVIN. Thanks. You too.

KAT. Is that one of Mom's dresses?

BRITTNEY. Yeah, how does it look?

(She spins around, showing it off.)

DAD. You look nice, sweetie.

KAT. Whatever.

MOM. *(To* **KAT***)* You need to get in there before everything is gone.

(**TRISH** *comes out of the den.*)

TRISH. Vikings are up by 17.

DAD. Yes!

MOM. Go Vikings!

DAD. Oh, Kevin, this is Trish.

KEVIN. Nice to meet you.

TRISH. Nice to meet you.

DAD. Kevin and I play golf together. He's joining us for dinner.

MOM. Excellent!

KAT. *(Unenthusiastic)* Great.

DAD. Can I get you a beer?

KEVIN. Sure.

DAD. *(Gets a beer at the bar)* Kevin has a computer company. Tell 'em what you do.

KEVIN. Oh, I design apps for i-phones and tablets. It's just a little company.

DAD. He's being modest. He just bought a big house on Lake Minnetonka. *(Pron. Mi-nah-ton-kah)*

TRISH. Oh, that's a nice area.

BRITTNEY. He's doing very well.

DAD. He's looking for a new receptionist. Sweetie, you should talk to him.

KEVIN. Oh, I don't know if Kat would wanna be a receptionist.

KAT. Seriously? You think he was talking to <u>me</u>?

DAD. I meant Brittney.

KAT. The Hooters Girl.

KEVIN. Oh, right, sorry.

BRITTNEY. Kat isn't dating anyone.

KAT. Whoa! Where did that come from?

BRITTNEY. Sorry, I just assumed. Are you?

KAT. I am in between boyfriends.

BRITTNEY. You dating anyone, Kevin?

KAT. Wow. I apologize for my sister.

KEVIN. That's okay.

(*To* **BRITT**) Yeah, it's complicated.

BRITTNEY. Oh, did you change your Facebook status?

(*To* **KAT**) We're Facebook friends.

KAT. I think my brain just exploded.

(**TRISH** *laughs.* **KAT** *notices.*)

DAD. (*Hands* **KEVIN** *the beer*) Brittney, let's ease up on Kevin, okay.

BRITTNEY. Oh, sorry. I just think everyone should find love.

KAT. Hah!

BRITTNEY. Oh, come on, you don't wanna get married some day?

KAT. Not while I still have hopes and dreams.

(**TRISH** *laughs.* **KAT** *looks at her.*)

TRISH. I'm sorry. You have the same sense of humor as your mother. She always made me laugh.

MOM. How sweet.

BRITTNEY. (*To* **KAT**) You're gonna find someone when you least expect it.

KAT. You mean like while I'm clipping my toenails in a public restroom? That would be unexpected. I need a re-fill. (*Goes to bar*)

MOM. Easy, now.

KAT. Just a small one.

BRITTNEY. You should try Match.com.

(**BRITTNEY** *goes to* **KAT**'s *computer on the coffee table and types something as* **KAT** *pours herself a drink, her back to* **BRITTNEY**. **MOM** *looks over* **BRITT**'s *shoulder at the computer screen.*)

KAT. Why are you still talking?

BRITTNEY. It's easy.

KAT. Britt, I am not in the market right now.

MOM. Why not?

BRITTNEY. Wait a minute. You're already on Match.com. "Looking for a man, any age, any income, any height or weight."

KAT. Turn that off.

BRITTNEY. Your problem is you're playing hard to get.

(**KAT** *puts her drink down and hurries over to* **BRITT**.)

KAT. I will stab you in the face.

(**KAT** *shuts the computer then looks at everyone staring at her. There's an awkward pause.*)

MOM. Awkward.

DAD. (*Changing the subject*) So… Kevin…how are your folks?

KEVIN. They're good. I was just visiting them when you called.

KAT. (*To* **DAD**) You just called him to come over, just now?

DAD. Kevin was quite the star in high school. Weren't you the captain of the football team?

KEVIN. I'm not sure if that's saying much. We didn't have a very good team.

(**MOM** *whispers something to* **KAT**.)

KAT. I played the clarinet in band.

DAD. (*Smiles at* **KAT**, *then to* **KEVIN**) Weren't you the Homecoming King?

KEVIN. That was not my idea.

BRITTNEY. All the girls liked Kevin. They still do.

(**MOM** *whispers again to* **KAT**.)

KAT. I was President of the Math Club.

BRITTNEY. (*Smiles at* **KAT**, *then to* **KEVIN**) Any good homecoming memories?

KAT. 3.14159265358979323…

(Everyone looks at KAT.*)*

That's Pi to 17 decimal places.

*(*MOM *gives her two thumbs up.)*

KEVIN. *(After a few uncomfortable beats)* Yeah, umm, my favorite homecoming memory was when someone buried a weather balloon under the end zone. During the 4th quarter the balloon inflated, rising out of the ground, above the crowd. When it got above the visitors' side, it popped, dumping thousands of pieces of paper that said "Release the Kracken!"

(He laughs.) I have no idea what that means.

KAT. It's from "Clash of the Titans."

TRISH. Who did it?

KEVIN. Oh, they never found out. It was awesome. It must have been on a timer.

KAT. Actually it was a remote control.

KEVIN. That was you!?

KAT. I will neither confirm nor deny it.

KEVIN. Well, whoever did it was a genius.

KAT. Okay, it was me.

MOM. I'm so proud of my daughter, the felon.

KAT. *(Changing the subject)* Enough about me.

MOM. No, stay on topic! You have him!

KAT. *(Ignoring* MOM*)* Trish works in home care.

MOM. *(Groans)* Ohh!

KEVIN. Really?

TRISH. I was an E-R nurse for 15 years, then went into home care.

KAT. *(To* TRISH*)* Would you like a glass of wine?

TRISH. No, I'll just stick with the Diet Coke. Thanks.

KAT. There's a real nice cabernet.

TRISH. Yeah, I'm not really a drinker.

BRITTNEY. I'll have one.

KAT. *(To* KEVIN, *ignoring* BRITT*)* Trish took care of Mom after the accident.

MOM. She was great.

BRITTNEY. I'll get it.

(Goes to get some wine.)

KAT. What exactly happened to Mom? I mean, how did she die?

DAD. Honey, I don't think this is the right time for this.

KAT. I'd like to know.

MOM. Why?

KAT. I wasn't there.

TRISH. Well, in the accident she suffered a head injury. As you know, she was in the hospital for three weeks. She was stable enough to go home, and that's when I came in to help care for her. She was lucid for a few more weeks while I was with her, but then she took a turn for the worse.

DAD. I told you all this.

KAT. I know. I just wanted to hear Trish's thoughts.

TRISH. She suffered a subdural hematoma.

BRITTNEY. What's a–

KAT. A blood clot.

TRISH. She went into a coma and three days later she was gone.

KEVIN. You know, I'm just gonna go across the street to my parent's and, ahh…get something I forgot. I'll be back in a little bit.

(He leaves.)

MOM. *(To* KEVIN, *following him)* No, no, don't go!
(He's gone, she stops. To KAT*)* Oh, you just lost him. Good work.

DAD. Kat, honey, it's just not appropriate to talk about that in front of guests.

KAT. Just a few more questions, then I'm done, I promise. Was it confirmed that she was brain dead?

DAD. You know it was.

TRISH. Yes, unfortunately.

MOM. What's the point?

KAT. Do you know what triggered the hematoma?

TRISH. No. It could have been a number of things.

KAT. *(Testing* **TRISH***)* And it all started with a drunk driver.

TRISH. *(Uncomfortable)* Yeah… Well, I guess I should probably get dinner started. *(Starts for the kitchen, then stops)* Oh, I forgot something in the car.

(She heads for the door.)

DAD. I'll get it.

TRISH. Oh, thanks. The grocery bag in the back seat.

DAD. I'll be right back.

*(***DAD*** goes out the door, and heads to the car.)*

MOM. *(To* **KAT***)* You're losing focus, here. Let's get back to the mission.

KAT. *(To* **TRISH***)* So, how did you like being a nurse?

TRISH. Oh, I loved it. It was incredibly rewarding.

KAT. Mom was a nurse.

TRISH. Yeah, she told me.

KAT. I guess Dad likes being around care givers.

BRITTNEY. Being a Hooters Girl is like being a nurse.

MOM. I was thinking the exact same thing.

KAT. So, why go from being an E-R nurse to home care?

TRISH. Well, being an E-R nurse is very stressful, and I needed to take a break from that for awhile.

BRITTNEY. You know, being a Hooters Girl is really stressful, too. "Where's my hot sauce?!" Gah. Get it yourself, right?!

MOM. She plays it so straight.

KAT. *(Looks at* **MOM***)* What was Mom like before going into the coma? Was she sad or angry, or…?

TRISH. Oh…well…actually, she was upbeat, positive. Really, kind of inspirational.

(**DAD** *enters with a bag of groceries.*)

(*To* **DAD**) Oh, good, you found it. Thanks.

KAT. You know what, I need to make a call. I'll be right back. (*Looking out the window, to* **TRISH**) Oh, I like your Prius. Is it new?

TRISH. Oh, thanks. It's about a year old.

KAT. Oh. What did you used to drive?

TRISH. A Camry.

KAT. Oh, yeah, those are nice, too.

(**KAT** *goes out on the porch with* **MOM**, *sits on the bench, takes out her cell phone and pretends to talk into it.*)

DAD. (*To* **TRISH**) Need any help? I'm a good cook.

TRISH. (*Taking the groceries, playful*) Yes, you are, but we're not making microwave hotdogs.

BRITTNEY. Why don't you two just get a room?

TRISH. (*Laughs*) Oh, that's funny.

DAD. Why is that funny?

TRISH. (*Serious*) Oh, no, I didn't mean "ha ha" funny, I meant–

(*Laughs, quickly changes*) yes I did. I totally meant that.

BRITTNEY. It's like watching senior citizen porn.

TRISH. (*Smiles, to* **DAD**) Go watch the game.

(**DAD** *goes in the den.* **TRISH** *and* **BRITT** *go in the kitchen. As* **BRITT** *goes in, she looks back at* **KAT** *on the porch, talking into her cell phone, sitting on the bench next to* **MOM**.)

MOM. Why would you ask those questions about my last days in front of Kevin?

KAT. What does it matter? I'm not gonna marry him. (*Looks inside, sees no one in the living room and puts away her cell phone*)

MOM. How do you know? That could be my mission, to get you and Kevin together.

KAT. I thought it was resolving my issues with Dad.

MOM. It could be either one.

KAT. Well, how will you know which one it is?

MOM. When you accomplish the right one and I'm gone.

KAT. Well, Kevin's not the mission. He tortured me in sixth grade.

MOM. He what?

KAT. He sat behind me in class and pulled my pigtails. That's elementary school water boarding.

MOM. That's because he liked you.

KAT. Can we please change the subject.
    (Changing it) Trish. What's going on, there? Why is she here?

MOM. She's making dinner. It's no big deal.

KAT. Have you ever seen her drink alcohol?

MOM. No, why?

KAT. It's just that every time you mention drunk driver, she can't leave the room fast enough.

MOM. Good to know. Thank you. Moving on.
    (Changing the subject) You know, I think you and Kevin would be good together.

KAT. *(Groans)* Oh, are we back on that?

MOM. Sometimes you need to put yourself out there, and just go for it.

KAT. Yeah, I know, seize the day, carpe diem and other Latin beer commercials.

MOM. That's right. You need to make yourself available. Your eggs won't fertilize themselves, you know.

KAT. You're dead and you're still trying to control my life.

MOM. When did I control your life?

KAT. Remember when I couldn't get a date for prom?

MOM. *(Thinks)* Which year?

KAT. Senior year. You set me up on a prom date with my first cousin. Then you went to chaperone it so I wouldn't make out with my <u>first cousin</u>! What are we in Appalachia?

MOM. He was <u>French</u>!

KAT. New topic.

MOM. Wait, maybe you're gay. Of course, with your pants and your comfortable shoes.

KAT. Mom! Just because I wear the uniform, doesn't mean I march in the band.

MOM. *(Thinks)* You <u>did</u> march in the band.

KAT. I know, but not <u>that</u> band. Err!

(She sees **KEVIN** *in the distance.)* Oh, fungus, Kevin's coming back.

MOM. My future son in law.

*(***KAT*** *shoots her a look)* What?

KAT. Why would Dad invite him over?

MOM. I don't know, but I'm all for it. He could help me get my wings, and you might find love. Win, win.

*(***KEVIN*** *approaches, carrying a bottle of wine.* **KAT** *and* **MOM** *watch him approach.)*

KEVIN. Oh, hey, thanks for the offer, there, Mrs. Norquist, but I don't think your husband would like it if you showed me your new thong.

(Looks back at **MRS. NORQUIST***)*

<u>Oh, she did! She did! Oh!</u>

KAT & MOM. *(Looking at her thong)*
<u>Ohhh!</u>

*(***KEVIN*** *gags from the sight of her thong, and so does* **KAT** *and* **MOM***. He turns toward* **KAT***, rubbing his eyes.)*

KEVIN. I will never un-see that.

KAT. *(Rubbing her eyes)* I'm gonna have to bleach my eyeballs.

MOM. That was painful, and I'm dead.

(**KEVIN** sits on the bench by **KAT** with **MOM** sitting in between them.)

KEVIN. Hey, congratulations, by the way.

KAT. For what?

KEVIN. Well, you seem to be doing really well, I mean, Dartmouth, M.I.T., that's pretty cool, and an engineer. Too bad you hate men.

KAT. Funny… So, did my dad tell you I was an engineer?

KEVIN. Brittney keeps me updated.

KAT. Facebook.

KEVIN. Yeah. Hey, sorry again about your mom.

KAT. Thanks.

KEVIN. She was always really nice to me.

MOM. I like him.

KEVIN. You know, I thought I'd see you at the class reunion.

KAT. Oh, yeah, I was busy that night jamming an ice pick into my cornea.

(**KEVIN** *mimes jamming an ice pick into his eye, blood gushing out, with sound effects and everything. Sensing with* **KAT** *that he's gone too far, he stops.*)

KEVIN. Too much?

(**KAT** *smiles. It's awkward. Changing the subject.*) It's weird how we grew up across the street from each other but never really hung out.

KAT. Well, you had all your girl friends and I had Math Club.

KEVIN. Oh, there weren't that many. It was Cindy and then Joanne.

KAT. Actually, it was Maggie then Joanne then Cindy then Carol then back to Cindy. But I really wasn't keeping track.

MOM. Hah!

KEVIN. I thought you didn't remember me.

KAT. Yeah, well, that's all I remember.

KEVIN. When's my birthday?–

KAT. June 8th.

    (Busted) Dangit!

KEVIN. Do you still have the telescope in your bedroom?

MOM. Busted.

KAT. What telescope?! No! Shut up! You knew about that?!

KEVIN. Why do you think I kept my blinds open?

MOM. *(Channeling Ed McMahon)* Hey-oh!

KAT. *(Embarrassed)* Oh, my gosh. I just wanna crawl into a hole.

KEVIN. Hey, I have a confession to make.

MOM. A confession!

KEVIN. I had a crush on you in elementary school.

MOM. I knew it!

KAT. Are you messing with me?

KEVIN. No, I'm serious.

KAT. I thought you hated me.

KEVIN. Why would you think that?

KAT. You pulled my pigtails.

KEVIN. That's because I liked you.

MOM. I told you.

KAT. I wanted to kill you. I actually plotted to poison you with Elmer's Glue.

KEVIN. It's poisonous?

KAT. I thought it was, but then Jimmy Hansen ate all the glue and he didn't die, so I guess not.

KEVIN. Elmers Glue tasted so good.

KAT. I know, didn't it?

KEVIN. I really liked you. All thru high school. But you were so intimidating.

KAT. I intimidated you? Captain of the football, hockey and baseball teams?

KEVIN. Yeah, you intimidated all the guys.

KAT. I was a wall flower. I never went on any dates.

KEVIN. Well, they didn't ask you out because they felt stupid around you.

KAT. Oh, those morons!

KEVIN. I mean, you were the smartest kid in high school. Weren't you valedictorian?

KAT. I was second, salutatorian. Emily Chambers was valedictorian. She was in theater! Here I am, taking math and physics and chemistry and she's taking theater. I mean, how do you get a bad grade in theater? Seriously. It's totally subjective! "To be or not to be. That is the question." Really?! That's the question?! I have a question. Where's Emily now? Doing dinner theater in Duluth, that's where. Way to go, Emily. Would you like fries with that? I got your fries right here, sister!!

(She catches herself, subtly turns away from **KEVIN** *so he can't see, and does a smaller version of her zen-like motion with her hands to calm down)*

KEVIN. Little upset about that?–

KAT. Not at all.

KEVIN. Is that why you were a math major? You didn't like the subjective courses?

KAT. Yeah, I've always been bad at b-s-ing, and you can't b-s in math. It's either right or it's wrong. There's no in between.

KEVIN. Isn't there partial credit?

KAT. Partial credit is for weenies.

KEVIN. I remember competing against you in elementary school.

KAT. I'm sorry, what?

KEVIN. I mean, it's one thing to be the smartest kid in class, but you were the fastest in the 50 yard dash, and that angered me.

KAT. I angered you?

KEVIN. I was obsessed with you. I mean, I made it my life goal to beat you in school, yet I was wildly attracted to you.

MOM. <u>Kiss him!</u>

(**KAT** *shoots her a look.*)

<u>Kiss him right now!</u>

KAT. Mom!

KEVIN. Excuse me?

KAT. *(Covering)* Mom…always pushed me to do things I was uncomfortable with.

KEVIN. I just wanna thank you.

KAT. For what?

KEVIN. For making me a better 6th grader.

MOM. <u>Kiss him or I will!!</u>

KAT. Stop it!

KEVIN. Okay, I'll stop.

KAT. No, you can keep going.

KEVIN. I like that you're so honest.

KAT. I have prescription strength deodorant.

KEVIN. Okay, not that honest.

KAT. Then I won't tell you about my webbed feet.

KEVIN. I bet no one's ever told you how pretty you are.

KAT. *(Thinks)* Okay, is that a compliment, or…?

KEVIN. Oh, that sounded terrible.

KAT. Yeah, little bit.

KEVIN. I'm sorry, I'll shut up.

KAT. Okay.

KEVIN. I just thought you'd be married by now.

KAT. Oh, you're still talking.

KEVIN. I mean, you're smart and successful and grounded.

KAT. Okay, go on.

KEVIN. You wear comfortable shoes and you don't feel pressure to trim your eyebrows.

KAT. And, you can stop.

KEVIN. Would you like to, maybe have lunch some time? You know, catch up on the old days?

MOM. Yes, she would.

KAT. What about your "it's complicated" relationship? Oh, my gosh, I hate Facebook. Created by a geek from Harvard.

KEVIN. Yeah, umm…when I said, "it's complicated," what I meant was that work has been a priority to me, and not dating.

KAT. So, you don't have a girl friend.

KEVIN. Not currently.

KAT. "Not currently?"

KEVIN. No. So, you wanna have lunch some time?

KAT. Yeah, I don't think I can do that.

MOM. What in the hot fudge are you doing?

KEVIN. Oh, I'm sorry, I didn't mean to be so forward.

(**DAD** *comes out of the den and sees* **KAT** *and* **KEVIN** *outside on the porch.*)

KAT. No, no, it's just that I'm going to Somalia for a couple years.

KEVIN. Wow. Let me know where to send the ransom check.

(**DAD** *opens the door and leans out.*)

DAD. Packers scored. Vikings are up by 10 in the third quarter.

MOM. Hang in there, Vikes!

KEVIN. *(Holding up a bottle of wine.)* Happy birthday!

(**BRITT** *enters the living room and starts taking out plates from under the bar to set the table.*)

DAD. *(Takes the bottle)* Thank you! Hey, why don't you grab a beer and go check out the game in the den.

KEVIN. Sounds good.

(He goes inside. To **BRITT***)* Need any help?

BRITTNEY. *(Smiles at* **KEVIN***)* No, I'm good.

(**KEVIN** *grabs an appetizer from the dining table and a beer, then goes in the den as* **BRITTNEY** *takes out silverware and glasses for dinner.*)

(**KAT** *is about to go in.*)

DAD. Oh, Kat, can I talk to you for a minute?

MOM. Here's your chance to make up.

KAT. Sure. What's up?

DAD. It's about Trish.

KAT. *(Uneasy)* Okay.

DAD. Alright, umm, well…do you like her?

KAT. I don't know. She seems nice enough. Why?

MOM. She's wonderful. We love Trish.

DAD. She's been very helpful since your mom died. I mean, over the past eight months, Trish has really been there for me.

MOM. She's an angel.

KAT. So, are you dating her, or…?

MOM. Don't be silly.

DAD. Well, I wanted to talk to you about that.

MOM. About what?

(**DAD** *looks in and sees* **BRITT.**)

DAD. You know, I'd like Britt to hear this. Let's go in. *(He goes in with* **KAT** *and* **MOM.**)

MOM. What's going on? What are we doing? What's happening?

DAD. Umm, Britt, honey, will you join us?

(*He leads them down stage, away from the kitchen.*)

BRITTNEY. Sure, what's up?

DAD. Well, it's very important to me that you two like Trish.

BRITTNEY. I do like Trish.

DAD. Good. You see, we've been dating for about 7 months…

MOM. Oh, crap.

DAD. And she's very special to me, and while you're both here, I was hoping to get your blessing.

KAT. Blessing? For what?

MOM. Oh, this is not good.

(**TRISH** *comes out of the kitchen.* **DAD** *doesn't see her.*)

DAD. I'd like to propose to Trish.

(**TRISH** *and* **MOM** *both grab their hearts and faint at the same time.* **DAD** *looks over at* **TRISH** *on the ground.*)

(*Blackout*)

End of Act I

ACT II

(**DAD** *and* **BRITT** *are hovering around* **TRISH**, *who's on the floor on her back.* **KEVIN** *is holding a glass of water.* **TRISH** *and* **MOM** *are coming to.* **KAT** *is by* **MOM**, *who is also on her back.*)

MOM. *(Coming to)* I'm sorry, did he just propose to Trish, or did I dream that?

DAD. *(To* **TRISH***)* Trish, Trish…was that a "no?"

MOM. Oh, crap.

DAD. Trish, are you okay? Say something.

TRISH. We should probably eat sometime.

MOM. Homewrecker!

DAD. Let's do that later when you're feeling better.

MOM. I'm not ready for this!

TRISH. I'm making meatloaf.

BRITTNEY. It's so good.

DAD. We'll have it later.

(To **KEVIN***)* She makes the best meatloaf.

MOM. I really hate her!

KAT. Mom made a pretty good meatloaf.

MOM. "Pretty good?"

TRISH. And mashed potatoes.

BRITTNEY. I love mashed potatoes.

TRISH. You use whole milk, right?

BRITTNEY. Of course.

(They help **TRISH** *up into the easy chair.* **MOM** *gets up, slowly.*)

TRISH. I mean, skim milk? Why bother? It's like driving a sports car with an automatic transmission.

DAD. She's still a little groggy. Here.

> (**KEVIN** *hands* **DAD** *the glass of water,* **DAD** *hands it to* **TRISH** *who takes a drink.*)

MOM. I'm a giver, I'm just not ready to give up my husband!

TRISH. I'm making birthday cake, too, from scratch. German Chocolate.

DAD. She makes the best I've ever had.

MOM. Oh, I could just die!

KAT. Mom's was pretty good.

MOM. You need to work on your adjectives.

DAD. *(To* **TRISH***)* Are you okay?

TRISH. Yeah, I'm fine.

DAD. Okay, I know that it must be a surprise to everyone, the whole proposal thing.

KAT. Yeah.

MOM. New mission! Stop the wedding!

DAD. *(To* **KEVIN***)* Sorry to bring you into this.

KEVIN. Oh, hey, no problem. Really.

MOM. She's too young and too pretty and too alive!

DAD. *(To* **TRISH***)* I didn't mean for you to hear that until I talked to my daughters, but since you did, and I'm not sure what direction you were going with the fainting thing…any thoughts?

TRISH. Wow. Umm, this is a little awkward for me. I mean, we haven't even talked about it… What, umm, what do your daughters think?

MOM. Kat, say something.

KAT. Well, it hasn't even been a year since Mom died, and it seems like you're kind of rushing into it, you know. I… I feel like we're just forgetting Mom. I mean, we didn't even have a memorial for her.

BRITTNEY. She's right. Let's do it. Let's have a memorial for Mom.

KAT. Right now?

BRITTNEY. Right now. We'll go around and everyone who wants to, will share a fond memory of Mom.

KAT. Seriously? Right now?

DAD. Honey, I don't know if that's such a good idea–

BRITTNEY. I'll go first. Okay, umm….okay, Mom was a great cook, right, and she taught me everything I know. About cooking. Not about sex. I learned that from – (looks at **DAD**) inappropriate, inappropriate. Alright… And I just hope I can make Mom proud of my cooking and my Hooter skills, even tho she's in a better place right now.

(She looks up.)

MOM. Not quite.

BRITTNEY. *(Looking up)* And while we're talking, I just pray that Manson gets his dream job cleaning monkey cages at the Como Park Zoo.

DAD. Thank you. Very nice. Very nice.

MOM. That <u>was</u> nice.

*(**KEVIN** starts to slowly move to the hallway to slip out before his turn.)*

BRITTNEY. Alright, who's next? Kevin?

KEVIN. *(He stops and turns back. Put on the spot)* Oh, okay… umm…your mom was great, and I remember one day, I was about 10, and I fell off my bike and just trashed my elbow. It was bleeding, horrible. I thought I was gonna die. Your mom saw me and she ran out of the house with bandages and antiseptic, which made it feel even worse, you know.

*(He looks at **DAD** and **KAT**)* But I guess you have to go thru a little pain in order to start the healing…

*(**DAD** and **KAT** look at each other)* I really felt that your mom saved my life that day.

MOM. I like this.

BRITTNEY. *(Smiling at **TRISH**)* Trish?

TRISH. Oh, well, umm…she was always so kind to me, the short time I knew her. She had a great sense of humor, never felt sorry for herself. I think I was more concerned about her than she was. And one day she said to me, "Are you afraid?… Because I'm not."… She was brave until the end.

MOM. It is so hard to hate her.

DAD. I will always truly miss Peggy. She meant the world to me. We were married for 35 years, and she was my best friend, and… I'm sorry.

(He gets emotional, and can't finish.)

BRITTNEY. *(Puts her hand on his shoulder)* That was nice.

KAT. *(Unemotional)* Okay, umm… Sometimes I feel like Mom is still with us.

MOM. *(Raising her hand)* Yo.

KAT. She, umm…she inspired me, and encouraged me to be the best person I could be. She went to all my band concerts and math-bees, and I always appreciated that. And if she were here, I would say, "thank you, Mom, for being a great friend and inspiration." I just don't understand that, if there is a God, why would they take someone like Mom. It makes no logical sense to me. So, I can only conclude that there is no God.

MOM. *(Disappointed)* Oh, Kat.

BRITTNEY. I disagree.

DAD. Okay, umm, well, thank you for sharing, everyone.

BRITTNEY. Let's have a seance!

DAD. Yeah, sweetie, I would prefer if we could get back to me and Trish.

BRITTNEY. Oh, I just got a text from Manson.
(Reads it) "I love you more than all the lake trout in the ocean."

KEVIN. *(Thinks)* Isn't lake trout a fresh water–

KAT. Don't. Just, don't.

BRITTNEY. Dad, I say go for it. Get married.

DAD. *(To* **TRISH***)* See? They're okay with it.

(**MOM** *shoots a look at* **KAT**, *clearing her throat, "say something!")*

KAT. *(What about me?)* Helloooo.

TRISH. I think you might wanna talk to Kat.

(**BRITT** *is looking at her cell phone.)*

BRITTNEY. Oh, my gosh. Manson just proposed to me!

DAD. He what?!

KAT. What did he say?

BRITTNEY. "Marry me, sugar tits."

(Swoons) Ohh. So romantic.

MOM. New mission! Get rid of Manson!

DAD. Sweetie, marriage is a big commitment.

BRITTNEY. You did it. You're gonna do it again. I mean, if Trish says "yes."

TRISH. *(Feeling awkward, like she's prying on family business)* You know, I think I'm gonna go check on dinner.

KEVIN. Yeah, and I think I'll just go in the den, and… *(Points to the den)*

DAD. Sorry about that. Just a little family stuff.

(**KEVIN** *and* **TRISH** *overlap in dialogue.)*

KEVIN. Totally understand. Go right ahead. Take your time.

TRISH. No problem at all. Don't worry about it. Keep going.

(Overlapping dialogue ends.)

(**TRISH** *and* **KEVIN** *stand there for another awkward beat, then, at the same time,* **TRISH** *goes into the kitchen and* **KEVIN** *goes into the den.)*

DAD. Sweetie, I just think you should get established first. Like Kat.

BRITTNEY. But, Dad, I love Manson.

DAD. Honey, love is blind, but marriage is a real eye opener.

MOM. Exactly! Wait, what?

BRITTNEY. I don't see the difference between my love for Manson and your love for Trish.

DAD. *(To* **KAT***)* A little help. Anyone?

KAT. Dad, I think Brittney would be smart to marry Manson–

(She quickly laughs) I'm sorry, I couldn't land it.

BRITTNEY. I wanna have babies while it's still cool.

KAT. Is it cool to have prison babies? I forget.

DAD. Sweetie, your life is over when you have kids.

KAT. Thanks.

DAD. *(To* **KAT***)* I didn't mean that in a bad way.

(To **BRITTNEY***)* Look, you don't even know this guy.

BRITTNEY. We're soul mates. Like you and Trish.

*(***KEVIN*** comes out of the den to grab an appetizer.)*

DAD. Wait, are you pregnant?

BRITTNEY. No, I'm on The Pill.

*(Hearing that, ***KEVIN*** turns and goes back in the den.)*

DAD. <u>Not</u> what I wanted to hear.

KAT. Whenever I think about wanting kids, I eat lunch at Chuckie Cheese. That's <u>my</u> birth control.

BRITTNEY. I thought your personality was your birth control.

MOM. Can we please get back to Dad and Trish.

KAT. Dad, can we talk somewhere?

DAD. Sure, let's go outside.

*(***DAD*** and **KAT** head toward the door.)*

BRITTNEY. What about me?

DAD. Don't answer Manson. Ever.

BRITTNEY. *(Groans)* Ohh!

*(***KAT*** and **DAD** exit to the porch. **MOM** follows. **BRITT** goes in the kitchen.)*

MOM. *(Looking back at* **BRITT***, as she exits.)* What are you up to, Brittney.

DAD. I'm sorry I didn't talk to you about Trish.

KAT. Yeah, well, what else is new?

MOM. You need to change his mind.

DAD. I know it seems a little soon to be getting re-married.

MOM. Ya think?

KAT. Dad, it's just that, how long have you known Trish?

MOM. Good question.

DAD. I met her after the accident. She came in to help Mom.

MOM. It hasn't even been a year.

KAT. Did you have an affair with her while Mom was alive?

DAD. No! Absolutely not! I haven't slept with her yet.

KAT. Really?

DAD. I'm serious. I haven't even seen her naked.

MOM. Don't wanna hear this.

DAD. I mean we made out and everything.

KAT. Ewe.

MOM. Please stop.

DAD. For, like, hours.

KAT & MOM. Ohhh.

DAD. A little over the blouse stuff.

KAT & MOM. OHHH!!

DAD. But nothing else.

KAT. Wow. Old school.

DAD. I just want to be respectful.

KAT. So, let me ask, do you feel like you need to get married?

DAD. Well, I feel like… I'm lonely… I miss your mom.

MOM. *(Loving)* Ohh.

KAT. Well, why don't you just date?

DAD. What, and waste all my Viagra?

(**MOM** *laughs.*)

KAT. Dad! Seriously.

DAD. Too soon?

KAT. That joke will always be too soon.

DAD. Sorry.

MOM. It was kinda funny.

KAT. I just don't understand why you can't wait a little longer. I mean, do you really know her?

DAD. Like in what way?

KAT. Well, she shows up after the accident to help Mom. How did she find out about Mom?

DAD. I don't know. I think from a nursing service.

KAT. Is she an alcoholic?

DAD. Why would you say that?

KAT. She doesn't drink.

DAD. So?

KAT. So, why does she show up out of the blue to help Mom?

DAD. What do you mean?

KAT. I mean, was it out of guilt?

DAD. I don't know what you're saying.

KAT. Did you see the type of car that hit you?

(**BRITT** *comes out of the kitchen.*)

DAD. No, it happened too fast.

KAT. Did they ever find the drunk driver?

DAD. No. Wait, you don't think that Trish?… I'm gonna pretend I didn't hear that.

(**BRITT** *sticks her head out the door.*)

BRITTNEY. Are you two done yet? We have guests, you know.

(**DAD** *looks at* **KAT.**)

KAT. (*To* **DAD**) Go ahead. I'll be right in.

(**DAD** *goes inside, and goes in the den.* **BRITT** *starts setting the table.*)

MOM. You think Trish was the drunk driver that hit us?

KAT. She's got a car that's about a year old. The other one could have been trashed in the accident. She feels guilty and she shows up after the accident to help you. It's not impossible.

MOM. You are getting into dangerous territory, young lady.

KAT. You know, you're right. All I have to do is get thru another hour of this and I can leave. That's my goal. Not to argue for another hour, then I'm outta here.

MOM. You're just giving up on resolving your differences with Dad?

KAT. I can't fix that! No one can!

(KAT *takes a deep breath and does a zen-like movement with her hands.*)

MOM. So you're not gonna help me complete my mission?

KAT. I don't even know what the mission is anymore. Get me and Dad together, get me and Kevin together, get rid of Trish, stop Brittney from getting married.

MOM. Well, you might just have to complete each one of 'em. You'll figure it out.

KAT. The Theory of Relativity is easier to figure out.

MOM. Which you did.

(KAT *shoots* MOM *a look*) Alright, let's make it simple. How about if you just help Dad "see the light" with Trish. He's still in mourning. Dad doesn't even know what's best for him.

(DAD *and* KEVIN *come out of the den into the living room.*)

KAT. Is he still in mourning?

(MOM *doesn't answer. She goes inside with* MOM.)

DAD. Packers scored again. Vikings are only up by three.

BRITTNEY. Why do they make it so hard to be a Vikings fan?

KAT. So, Britt, are you gonna marry Manson, or what?

BRITTNEY. I'd like to.

DAD. Oh, for...what can I do to get you to just think about it for nine or ten years?

(**TRISH** *comes out of the kitchen.*)

BRITTNEY. Well, it's either get married, or pursue a career path.

KAT. By the way, what is your career path? Hooters girl, stripper and then meth lab attendant?

(**TRISH** *and* **KEVIN** *overlap in dialogue.*)

TRISH. *(Uneasy)* I think I'll just go back in the kitchen, and...

KEVIN. *(Uneasy)* You know, maybe I'll just go check on the game...

(*Overlapping dialogue ends.*)

(**TRISH** *and* **KEVIN** *start exiting to the kitchen and den.*)

DAD. *(Stopping* **TRISH** *and* **KEVIN***)* No, no, you can stay, you can stay.

BRITTNEY. I'm talking about my muffin top business.

KAT. You bake muffin tops. That's not a business.

DAD. They are good.

TRISH. Very good.

(**TRISH** *holds a plate of muffin tops out to* **KEVIN**. *He takes one, eats it, and likes it.*)

BRITTNEY. Thanks. I know how I can mass produce 'em. I just don't have the start-up capital.

KAT. Start-up capital? What are you, Donald Trump?

DAD. How much do you need?

BRITTNEY. Ten thousand dollars.

DAD & MOM. Ten thousand dollars!?

BRITTNEY. To buy an industrial stove, supplies and a refrigerator.

DAD. Sweetie, that's a lot of money.

BRITTNEY. Banks won't lend it to me. I can pay you back in six months. It's all in my business plan.

KEVIN. You have a business plan?

BRITTNEY. I have a letter of intent from Caribou Coffee for 3,000 muffin tops.

DAD. A letter of intent?

TRISH. Oh, I love Caribou Coffee.

MOM. Better than Starbucks.

BRITTNEY. They have 500 locations.

TRISH. Whoa.

KAT. How did you get a letter of intent from Caribou Coffee?

BRITTNEY. I met the CEO at Hooters.

KAT. That figures.

KEVIN. Rick Stevens?

BRITTNEY. Do you know him?

KEVIN. I play golf with him.

BRITTNEY. Cool. Well, one day I brought in my muffin tops to Hooters and Rick tried one and loved it, and it just went from there. I just have to deliver the muffins and I'll get paid in a month, 30 days net. If they sell at Caribou, the purchasing manager at Target will order 20,000. They're buddies.

MOM. That's good.

KAT. Are these guys real, or are they just shining you on?

BRITTNEY. They're real. You see, it's all about distribution. I mean, you can have the best muffins in the world, but if you don't have distribution, you don't have a business.

KEVIN. She's right.

KAT. Where did you learn this stuff?

KAT & BRITTNEY. Hooters.

MOM. Let's get back to Manson.

KAT. So, if you can come up with ten thousand dollars for your business, you'll hold off on marrying Manson?

BRITTNEY. Yeah, I'd be too busy. I wouldn't have time for a relationship.

KAT. My sister, the extortionist.

BRITTNEY. ZIP-IT!!

KEVIN. Can I see your business plan?

BRITTNEY. Yes, of course.

*(She grabs her purse, takes it out and hands it to **KEVIN**. **KEVIN** takes it in the den.)*

DAD. Kat, did you get a chance to look at your mom's things?

KAT. No, not yet.

DAD. Why don't you and Brittney go split it up.

KAT. Yeah, okay.

MOM. Finally.

KAT. *(To **BRITT**)* Come on, Donald.

*(**KAT** and **BRITTNEY** disappear into the hallway, followed by **MOM**.)*

*(**DAD** and **TRISH** sit on the couch.)*

DAD. Sorry I just sprung the whole proposal thing on you.

TRISH. Hey, no problem. It happens to me all the time.

DAD. So, what do you think?

TRISH. About marriage? Oh, gosh, I don't know.

DAD. You know, I love you, right? I mean, I've said it twice.

TRISH. *(Smiles)* And I love you, too, I just never thought it would go this far.

DAD. Well, if we both love each other, then why don't we get married?

TRISH. Well, I just think that maybe we should get to know each other a little better.

DAD. I can do that. What do you want to know?

TRISH. Well, it's not so much what I want to know, it's more like what you should know.

DAD. Okay, what should I know?

TRISH. *(Thinks)* Well, okay…umm…you know Peggy, she was so kind, and…well, it just wasn't fair that she died so young.

DAD. Yeah, I know.

TRISH. I feel horrible about that, and I need to tell you something that's been weighing on me for a long time.

DAD. Okay.

TRISH. I, ahh…oh, this is hard for me to say…

(She can't finish.) You know, I'm sorry. I'm just not prepared for this.

DAD. Do you love me?

TRISH. Yes. I love you with all my heart. That's not it.

DAD. What is it?

TRISH. I just… I need you to please take some time and think about whether this is what you really want.

DAD. I can do that.

TRISH. Thanks.

KEVIN. *(Entering from the den)* You know, this is a pretty good business plan. You oughta take a look at it.

*(Hands the business plan to **DAD**)*

DAD. I was hoping you wouldn't say that.

*(**KAT** comes out of the hallway wearing a sexy dress, carrying a small suitcase. **BRITT** and **MOM** follow. She sets the suitcase down and "presents herself.")*

KEVIN. Wow.

MOM. I know, right?

TRISH. You look beautiful.

KAT. Thanks.

BRITTNEY. I tried to get her to put on some makeup, but–

KAT. Baby steps.

BRITTNEY. *(To **KEVIN**)* Did you look at my business plan?

KEVIN. Yeah, it's good. I called Rick Stevens and he's looking forward to getting the first order.

KAT. So, it's real?

KEVIN. Yeah. And if Caribou and Target go well, she has good prospects at Cub Foods, Byerly's and Walmart. She has a well thought out plan.

KAT. You're talking about Brittney, right?

KEVIN. Tell me about the packaging.

BRITTNEY. Okay. I'm gonna name them after Mom. "Mom's Muffin Tops."

MOM. How sweet.

BRITTNEY. I'll put a photo of Mom on the package, maybe a close-up of her little muffin top.

(She grabs her "muffin top" area and parades around.) She would like that, right?

MOM. No, she would <u>not</u> like that.

KAT. She would <u>love</u> that.

BRITTNEY. I'm gonna donate a percent of the profits to the American Heart Association in Mom's name.

MOM. Oh, how nice.

BRITTNEY. Cause Mom had such a wonderful heart.

MOM. *(Touched)* Ohh.

BRITTNEY. So, what do you think, Dad?

DAD. Honey, I'm gonna need to think about it.

KEVIN. <u>I'll</u> lend you the money.

BRITTNEY. You will?

DAD. Kevin, I can't let you do that.

KEVIN. I want to. It's a good business plan. I can help, maybe develop a Mom's Muffin app.

BRITTNEY. Oh, my gosh. Thank you so much! *(She hugs him)*

DAD. Kevin, I can't possibly let you–

BRITTNEY. HE WANTS TO!!

KEVIN. I do. Maybe we can talk about an equity partnership.

BRITTNEY. Okay. Oh, I'm so excited. Thank you!

MOM. What a nice guy.

KAT. *(Jealous of* **BRITT** *and* **KEVIN***)* Oh, boy.

(Grabs the suitcase) I'm just gonna take this out to my car.

(She heads for the door.)

DAD. There's a lot more in there.

KAT. Yeah, I'll be back for the rest.

KEVIN. Can I join you?

KAT. *(Pleasantly surprised)* Sure.

> *(**KAT** goes outside with **KEVIN** to her car. **MOM** stays.)*

MOM. *(Realizing)* Wait, I'm still here. Dumping Manson wasn't the mission.

> *(Watching **KAT** leave with **KEVIN**)* Kevin! That's it! Wait! Wait! It's Kevin!

> *(**MOM** runs out and follows **KEVIN** and **KAT** to her car.)*

BRITTNEY. *(Re: **KEVIN** and **KAT**)* He likes her.

TRISH. Does she like him?

BRITTNEY. I think so. She just needs a little push.

TRISH. They look good together.

BRITTNEY. I know, don't they?

DAD. *(Uncomfortable)* Yeah, you know I think I'm gonna go check on the game. You two can…whatever.

> *(Goes into the den.)*

BRITTNEY. So, are you gonna say, "yes?"

TRISH. Oh, boy, I'd like to, I just…

BRITTNEY. Why wouldn't you?

TRISH. Oh, I don't know. I was married once before. It didn't go too well.

BRITTNEY. What happened?

TRISH. Oh, he was a bad guy, abusive alcoholic, I always had to clean up his messes.

BRITTNEY. But Dad is a good guy.

TRISH. I know. He's great. The best. I just need to get past a few things first.

> *(**KEVIN** and **KAT** come back to the porch with **MOM** and sit on the bench. **TRISH** and **BRITT** subtly spy on them.)*

MOM. Alright, Kat, here's your chance to complete the mission.

KEVIN. It seems like you have a lot of family stuff going on.

KAT. Yeah, it's like one big simultaneous equation with multiple variables.

KEVIN. Oh, so it's a math problem. Okay, so, what are the variables?

KAT. Dad, Mom, Trish, Britt, Manson, me…and you.

KEVIN. And does your family math problem get resolved?

KAT. Yes. I know, I'm just a romantic.

KEVIN. Uh huh. Question. Are you serious?

KAT. Everything can be explained with math. Even relationships. And best of all, math eliminates the need for emotions.

KEVIN. Yeah, not sure I buy the "relationships explained with math," theory.

MOM. Show your proof.

DAD. *(Coming out of den)* Game is all tied up–

> *(Sees **BRITT** and **TRISH** spying on **KAT** and **KEVIN**)*

BRITTNEY & TRISH. SHH!

KAT. You know the shortest distance between two points is a straight line.

MOM. Now, get me my wings!

KAT. *(Moves closer to him, seductive)* I mean, why beat around the bush, right? Just…go for it… *(Leaning in, about to kiss him, then stops)* That's the Pythagorean Theorem.

> *(She moves in for the kiss.)*

> *(Just before they kiss, Dad opens the door and leans out.)*

DAD. Drink anyone?

BRITTNEY & TRISH & MOM. *(Groaning)* OHH!

KAT. *(Annoyed at the interruption)* Sure.

MOM. I was this close!

> *(**KAT** smiles at **KEVIN** and they go in. Feeling a little hot under the collar from the near kiss, **KEVIN** takes off his sport coat.)*

BRITTNEY. We need to get some makeup on Kat, and do something with her hair.

KAT. No, no, I'm good, really.

BRITTNEY. Not your decision. Let's go.

KAT. Oh, crap.

(**BRITT** *leads* **KAT** *down the hallway, followed by* **TRISH**.)

MOM. (*Looking back at* **KEVIN**) This close!

(*She exits down the hallway.*)

(**DAD** *and* **KEVIN** *sit on the couch in the living room.* **KEVIN** *lays his coat over the back of the couch, between them.*)

DAD. (*Seeing the coat*) Feeling a little warm, there?

KEVIN. Yeah, little bit.

DAD. Hey, thanks for coming over, and for putting up with everything.

KEVIN. Are you kidding? This is the most entertainment I've had in weeks. How about you? How are you holding up?

DAD. Yeah, I'll be okay. I mean, it's a little tough. First time we've been together since the funeral.

KEVIN. Yeah, I can imagine.

DAD. So, do you think I'm making a mistake with Trish?

KEVIN. Oh, gosh, I am no expert in relationships.

DAD. Well, you seem to be doing pretty well with my daughter.

KEVIN. Kat? Oh, wow, this is actually a little awkward talking about my interest in your daughter.

DAD. No, that's good. I'm glad you're getting along. Look, I wanna give you this.

(*Hands* **KEVIN** *a check for $10,000*)

KEVIN. (*Looking at the check*) Ten thousand dollars? What's this for?

DAD. For investing in Brittney's business.

KEVIN. *(Hands the check back to* DAD*)* Oh, no, I want to invest in her company. I think she has a good plan.

*(*KAT, *wearing makeup with her hair looking nice, steps into the hallway with* MOM. DAD *slides the check into* KEVIN*'s coat pocket on the couch.* KAT *sees it. They don't see* KAT.*)*

DAD. Look, here's ten thousand dollars for Brittney, and if you can charm Kat into changing her mind about going to Somalia, there's another ten thousand in it for you.

*(*KAT, *shocked, turns and goes back down the hall.* MOM *stays.* KEVIN *looks at* DAD *for a few beats.)*

(Laughs) I'm just kidding. No one on earth can change Kat's mind about anything.

KEVIN. *(Laughs, as he takes the check out of his coat pocket)* Yeah, I get that impression.
(Hands the check back to DAD*)* Here, keep your money. This is something I wanna do.

DAD. You sure?

*(*KAT, *looking nice, comes out with another suitcase. She's angry.* KEVIN *turns and is impressed.)*

KEVIN. Hi.

KAT. *(Re: the suitcase)* Just more of Mom's stuff. I'm just gonna put it in my car. *(Heads to the front door with* MOM. KEVIN *gets up to open the door for* KAT.*)*

MOM. Don't judge him. Things are not always the way they appear.

*(*DAD *slips the check back into* KEVIN*'s coat pocket, without* KEVIN *noticing, as he watches* KAT *go outside.)*

*(*KAT *and* MOM *go outside and sit on the porch.* KAT *is not happy.*

*(*TRISH *and* BRITT *come out of the bedroom.)*

BRITTNEY. *(To* KEVIN*)* Kat looks good, doesn't she?

KEVIN. She looks great.

BRITTNEY. *(Sees* **KAT** *sitting on the porch)* What's she doing out there?

DAD. No idea. *(To* **TRISH***)* You need any help?

TRISH. No, I'm good.

DAD. Thanks for being such a trooper.

TRISH. Hey, no problem. You know <u>my</u> birthday's coming up.

DAD. *(Flirtatious)* I know, and I'm gonna do something very special for you.

BRITTNEY. Oh, my gosh, not in front of the children!

TRISH. Go watch the game.

> *(***TRISH** *smiles and goes in the kitchen.* **DAD** *gestures to* **KEVIN** *to follow him, and they exit to the den.)*

MOM. *(To* **KAT***)* You just gonna sit there and pout the rest of the day?

KAT. Pretty much.

> *(***BRITTNEY** *goes outside with* **KAT** *and* **MOM.** **KAT** *is despondent.)*

BRITTNEY. Why aren't you inside? What's going on?

KAT. Nothing.

MOM. Tell her.

BRITTNEY. I think Kevin really likes you.

KAT. What are we in fifth grade?

BRITTNEY. Do you like him?

KAT. *(Like a 5th grader)* Noooo.

MOM. Liar.

BRITTNEY. Really? Cause it seemed like you guys were hitting it off.

KAT. We're not.

BRITTNEY. Alright, what happened? He meant something to you. I saw it.

KAT. He's a guy. They're all the same. He means nothing to me.

MOM. Horse hockey.

BRITTNEY. Did he tell you I slept with him?

KAT. You slept with him?!

BRITTNEY. What? No! What just happened? Tourettes!

KAT. I will kill you!

(Goes to choke her, then pulls back, closes her eyes, takes a deep breath and does a zenlike movement with her hands) Use your words, not your fists.

BRITTNEY. I thought you said he didn't mean anything to you.

KAT. When have you ever listened to me?

(She grabs her purse and suitcase and storms off to her car. MOM stays.)

BRITTNEY. Wait, it's not what you think…

(KAT is gone.) And there she goes.

(BRITT goes inside.)

MOM. *(Watching KAT storm off)* My day is going in the same direction as the Vikings game.

(KEVIN comes out of the den.)

KEVIN. I can't believe the Vikings are down by three.

(MOM throws her hands up, "what did I just say.")

BRITTNEY. Kevin, you might wanna go and talk to Kat.

KEVIN. Why, what happened?

BRITTNEY. Oh, nothing that you can't fix.

KEVIN. Is something wrong?

BRITTNEY. Oh, I'll let you talk to her about that.

(KEVIN grabs his coat and puts it on as he goes outside on the porch by MOM.)

(BRITT exits to the kitchen, looking back at KEVIN as she goes.)

(KAT comes up to the house.)

MOM. You can fix this.

KEVIN. So…how's it going?

KAT. Are you like a gigolo or something?

MOM. This is fixing?

(**MOM**, *despondent, sits on the porch.*)

KEVIN. Alright, what's going on?

MOM. Don't say anything you'll regret.

KAT. I saw Dad give you ten thousand dollars to get Brittney to dump Manson, and then offer another ten thousand to "charm me" out of going to Somalia.

KEVIN. Well, first of all, I didn't take the money.

KAT. Really?

(**KAT** *reaches into* **KEVIN***'s coat pocket and takes out the ten thousand dollar check.*) What's this?

KEVIN. I gave this back to him. He must have put it back in my pocket.

(**KEVIN** *rips the check in half and hands it to* **KAT***.*)

KAT. Right.

KEVIN. I'm telling you the truth. I'm investing in Brittney's business because I think it can be successful.

KAT. So you can be a business partner with the sister that you <u>slept with</u>.

MOM. No filter.

KEVIN. Did she–?

KAT. Tell me the truth? Yeah, she told me the truth. More than I can say for you. All that crap about making you a better 6th grader. You had me going, there. You really did. I gotta give you credit. You played me like a <u>dirty banjo</u>.

KEVIN. *(Thinks)* Is that a saying?

KAT. Don't change the subject.

KEVIN. I mean, why does it have to be a <u>dirty</u> banjo?

KAT. It's my banjo. It can be dirty.

KEVIN. Yeah, but if <u>you're</u> the banjo, doesn't that make <u>you</u> the <u>dirty one</u>?

KAT. What are you, the logic police?

KEVIN. I didn't sleep with Brittney. And I was telling you the truth about 6th grade.

KAT. You didn't tell me the truth about the money, why should I believe you about Brittney?

KEVIN. Maybe you should ask Brittney.

KAT. So, you never went out with her?

KEVIN. Okay, we went out one time.

KAT. Ah ha!

KEVIN. As friends.

MOM. It's no use.

KEVIN. It seems like you have trust issues with men.

KAT. No, not at all. I don't trust men. There's no issue.

KEVIN. What happened, did you have a bad experience?

KAT. The last guy I dated faked his own death to get out of our relationship.

KEVIN. Trust me, we're just friends. Just ask her.

KAT. That's okay. I really don't care.

> (**BRITT** *comes out of the kitchen and sees* **KEVIN** *and* **KAT** *are still outside.*)

KEVIN. Look, I know this is a long shot, but I was just hoping I could convince you to maybe just...give me a chance.

KAT. I can't even look at you right now. Seriously.

KEVIN. Wow, your dad was right.

KAT. Really? You're gonna bring him into it?

KEVIN. Okay... I can see that I'm not gonna change your mind, so... I guess I should probably go... Look, do me a favor, would you, and, say goodbye to your dad.

> (**KEVIN** *leaves.* **BRITT** *sees* **KEVIN** *leaving, and knows something went wrong.*)

MOM. (*Watching* **KEVIN** *leave, waving*) Bye! So long, chance of getting into Heaven!

KAT. Sorry about that.

> (**KAT** *goes inside, followed by* **MOM**.)

MOM. Don't give up. We still have other missions.

BRITTNEY. *(Kidding)* So, when are you and Kevin getting married?

KAT. Wow. That's actually not bad coming from you.

BRITTNEY. Yeah, well, I'm full of surprises.

(**KAT** *sits on the couch and sets the torn check on the coffee table.*)

KAT. Yes, you are. Sleeping with Kevin. Big surprise. Huge.

BRITTNEY. Yeah, I wouldn't put a lot of negative energy into that.

KAT. You know what, it doesn't really matter. I'm fine with it.

MOM. No, you're not.

BRITTNEY. Don't just kick him to the curb. Kevin is a great guy.

KAT. Yeah, the son that Dad always wanted.

BRITTNEY. You have feelings for him and you're perfect together.

KAT. New topic… So, do you think Dad is doing the right thing with Trish, I mean, getting married so soon?

BRITTNEY. I just want him to be happy. I love Dad. He's like a father to me.

MOM. Wow.

KAT. And she's back.

(*Takes out a contract and a pen from her purse*)

Britt, I need you to do me a favor and sign something.

MOM. Are you bailing?

BRITTNEY. What is it?

KAT. Nothing. It's just something that says I was here.

MOM. So, you're giving up?

BRITTNEY. Alright, let me look at it.

(*Takes the pen and contract from* **KAT** *and reads it*)

KAT. Don't read it. Just sign it before Dad comes out.

BRITTNEY. Oh, no. No, no, no, no, no. I need to know what you did. *(She reads.)*

MOM. If you leave, I can't move on. You know that, right?

BRITTNEY. Oh, my gosh! You're a bad girl.

(Singing)

BAD GIRL, BAD GIRL, WHATCHA GONNA DO–

KAT. Would you knock it off.

DAD. *(Entering, before* **BRITT** *signs the contract)* What's going on?

BRITTNEY. Kat was ordered by the court to be here.

KAT. You are a walking suppository.

BRITTNEY. That's for dumping on me all day.

DAD. What's Brittney talking about?

*(***BRITT** *hands* **DAD** *the unsigned contract and pen. He reads it.)*

MOM. I am <u>not</u> having a good day.

KAT. I was really upset after the funeral and I got a speeding ticket.

DAD. *(Reading)* You punched a cop?!

KAT. It was just a shove.

DAD. It says you punched him.

KAT. Semantics.

MOM. Such a proud moment.

KAT. They said they would drop any charges if I went to anger management therapy and the therapist said I had to…

DAD. Had to spend time with your dad. You were ordered by the court to be here.

KAT. I'm sorry. I have issues, okay.

BRITTNEY. I'll just…

(Points to hallway) be in there if you need me.

*(***BRITT** *goes in the back bedroom.)*

MOM. *(To* **KAT***)* You can make this right before it's too late.

DAD. I don't know what to say… What happened to us?

KAT. Did you know that growing up I had an imaginary friend.

DAD. No, I didn't.

KAT. Yeah. I called him "Dad."

DAD. Okay, I know I was on call a lot and wasn't around sometimes, but do you have to punish me for the rest of my life?

MOM. He's reaching out to you.

KAT. I'm just going thru some stuff right now.

DAD. Look, I certainly don't want you to be here if you don't want to be here.

(He gets ready to sign the contract.)

MOM. Don't let him sign it!

KAT. What are you doing?

*(***DAD*** *signs the contract.)*

MOM. Ohh!

DAD. *(Handing it back to* **KAT***)*

Here you go. You're off the hook. Thank you for coming to my Birthday party. Oh, that's right, you were ordered by the court to be here. Thank the court for me.

KAT. I'm sorry. I tried.

DAD. Look, I still love you because you're my daughter, only a lot less than I loved you an hour ago. You better leave before it goes to zero.

(He goes in the den.)

MOM. Well, that's it, then. Boy, am I done. You can stick a fork right in my carcass.

(Slaps her butt)

KAT. I'm sorry I couldn't help you.

MOM. Don't give up on Dad. Everyone deserves a do-over.

KAT. I can't do it, okay? I can't resolve my differences with Dad, Kevin's not coming back, you didn't get your wings when Brittney dumped Manson. And I doubt if destroying Dad's relationship with Trish will get you into Heaven. What am I even doing? You're not even real. You're in my mind. I'm arguing with myself.

MOM. I'm not in your mind.

KAT. Oh, yeah? Then prove it. Show yourself to someone else. I need proof.

MOM. Sometimes you just need to have faith.

KAT. "Faith."

(Laughs) Huh. You get that on a Snapple cap?

MOM. Just have Dad "see the light" with Trish. That's all I ask.

KAT. What does that even mean?

MOM. You'll figure it out.

KAT. You know what, I can't do this anymore. It's making me nuts. I am this close to a straight jacket.

MOM. So, what are you saying? Do you want me to leave?

KAT. Yes. I'm sorry. I want you to leave.

MOM. Okay, fine. That's all you had to say.

(As MOM *exits)* Call me... Don't be a stranger.

*(*MOM *exits.* BRITT *enters from the hallway, carrying a suitcase.)*

BRITTNEY. Sorry about busting you like that.

(Sets the suitcase down)

KAT. Yeah, well, I guess I deserved it.

*(*KAT *starts to collect her things to leave.)*

BRITTNEY. Oh, yeah.

KAT. So, what will your boyfriend say about you two not getting married?

BRITTNEY. What boyfriend?

KAT. Manson, remember?

BRITTNEY. I don't know any Manson.

*(*KAT *turns her full attention on* BRITT.*)*

KAT. You don't have a boyfriend?!

BRITTNEY. Nope.

KAT. *(Thinks)* Holy crap! You made up the whole boyfriend thing to get the money for your business?!

BRITTNEY. Well, I actually did it to get Dad to re-think his relationship with Trish. I mean, you were so "hit him over the head" obvious. I just thought he needed a more subtle approach.

KAT. But you used it to get the ten thousand dollars.

BRITTNEY. Yeah, well there was that, too. But that was just an afterthought that turned into a bonus. I figured I was already there, I might as well take it over the goal line.

KAT. So…you're not dumb?

BRITTNEY. Dumb as a beaver.

KAT. *(Thinks, then corrects her)* Fox.

BRITTNEY. *(Flattered)* Why, thank you.

KAT. Really? You're still gonna play that?

BRITTNEY. As long as it keeps working for me.

KAT. Oh, my gosh. You are brilliant. I love-hate you.

BRITTNEY. Oh, I love-hate you, too. *(They hug)*

KAT. I guess if we hung out sometime I'd realize you're not a total idiot.

BRITTNEY. Oh, a compliment… Oh, and I did not sleep with Kevin.

KAT. You didn't?

BRITTNEY. No.

KAT. And you said you did because…?

BRITTNEY. I never said I slept with him. I just asked if he told you I slept with him.

KAT. *(Frustrated, "she tricked me with semantics.")* Oh, semantics!

BRITTNEY. You needed to get jealous and realize your feelings for him.

KAT. I have a whole new respect for you.

BRITTNEY. Thanks. So, what's been going on? You've been acting weird all day.

KAT. Oh, yeah. I have voices in my head.

BRITTNEY. You too!? Who talks to you?

KAT. Mom.

BRITTNEY. What does she say?

KAT. That I need to resolve my differences with Dad.

BRITTNEY. What differences?

KAT. Oh, I was angry about the accident, compounded by him not being around growing up.

BRITTNEY. What do you mean? He was around.

KAT. He never came to see any of my stuff.

BRITTNEY. *(Goes to her suitcase)* Are you serious?

KAT. You know what, it's no big deal, really. I'll get over it. Mom was there. That was enough.

(BRITT takes out a journal from her suitcase.)

BRITTNEY. You didn't know that Dad went to your events?

KAT. I'm okay with it, really.

BRITTNEY. *(Reads the journal)* "March 3rd. Kat was so good in the concert tonight. First chair clarinet. Dad came in late like he always does and sat in the back row. He was so proud of Kat. He filmed it and watched it three times when he got home."

KAT. What is that?

BRITTNEY. Mom's journal.

KAT. I didn't know she kept a journal.

(BRITT hands the journal to **KAT.** *She reads)* "May 16th. Kat won the Math-lympics. Dad was ecstatic. Afterwards, he handed out cigars, yelling, 'That's my daughter.' I don't know why he always sneaks in."

(She flips the page.) "June 6th, graduation. Kat gave the best speech out of all the presenters. Emily Chambers can suck it. Dad actually cried. A first for him."

BRITTNEY. Oh, doesn't that just make you wanna cry?

KAT. Where did you get this?

BRITTNEY. It was in the brown bag in the back of the closet.

KAT. *(Holding the journal. Unemotional)* This is what she wanted me to see.

BRITTNEY. Dad was really proud of you. That must make you feel good.

KAT. *(Unemotional)* Well, he should have said something. I don't know why he didn't.

BRITTNEY. You don't feel anything? No emotions? No heartstrings? Nothing?

KAT. *(Unemotional)* What do you want me to say?

BRITTNEY. *(She gets up)* Wow. You are a rock.

(She goes into the kitchen.)

KAT. And a rock feels no pain.

*(Stoic **KAT** can't hold it in any longer. The flood gates open. She breaks down and cries, showing emotions for the first time. **KAT** is alone for several moments, crying.)*

*(**DAD** comes out of the den.)*

DAD. Vikings are down by six–
   *(He sees **KAT**.)* Oh, you're still here…
   (He sees her crying.) What happened? Are you okay?

KAT. *(Holding the journal)* Why didn't you tell me you went to my concerts and math-bees?

DAD. Well, you didn't want me to go, remember? You said I embarrassed you. I think your exact words were, "I'm embarrassed to be seen in public with you."

KAT. Why does anyone listen to me?

DAD. Because what you say is important.

KAT. I never felt important. I mean, all my life you dote over Brittney, spending all your time with her.

DAD. Because Brittney is helpless!

BRITTNEY. *(Offstage) (From the kitchen)* I can hear you.

DAD. *(Bringing the volume down)* Please don't tell me you're envious of Brittney. You have so much confidence.

KAT. My confidence is a facade.

DAD. I don't understand that. With all your accomplishments.

KAT. I needed your approval. Some sort of validation from you that what I was doing was good. I just never felt that you were proud of me.

DAD. Oh, honey, I am so proud of you. All your success and recognition, and now helping others and literally saving lives. I couldn't be more proud.

KAT. *(Holding up journal)* I know that now. I just needed to hear it.

DAD. I'm sorry. I should have told you. I... I guess I didn't because, I don't know, because I wanted you to be strong and self sufficient. And you were. I mean, you were gonna succeed no matter what, and I never had to worry about you.

KAT. Sometimes I wanted you to worry about me, and lose sleep over me, and have mini strokes when I didn't call.

DAD. *(Raising his volume)* Honey, I didn't worry because I knew you could always take care of yourself.

BRITTNEY. *(Offstage) (From the kitchen)* I can take care of <u>my</u> self!

DAD. Oh, please!

    (To **KAT,** *lowering the volume)* What can I do to fix this?

KAT. I don't know. I'm still angry about Mom. Why did she have to die?

DAD. I don't know, honey. Everything happens for a reason. I just know that I loved her more than anything in the world, and...and I will always feel responsible for that night.

KAT. Then why move so quickly with Trish?

DAD. Because I have no one else. You're not around. I mean, I understand. You have your own life and I can't expect you to come over all the time.

KAT. You would want me to?

DAD. Yes, of course. I need you. What can I do to get you back?

KAT. *(Emotional)* I just want you to love me.

DAD. *(Emotional)* Oh, my gosh, I love you so much, honey. *(He hugs her.)* I know I should have said it more, and I wish I could do it over. I just…it would kill me if I ever lost you.

KAT. *(Emotional)* I'm sorry. I've just been so angry and mean and unfair to you and… I'm sorry.

DAD. Oh, honey, you don't have to apologize. It's okay, we'll be fine. We'll get thru it. We will.

KAT. You promise?

DAD. *(He holds out his little finger to do a "pinky promise".)* I promise…
(They lock pinkies.) So…am I doing the right thing with Trish, or is this like Brittney and Manson?

KAT. If she makes you happy, that's all that matters.

DAD. Thanks… So, what's going on with you and Kevin?

KAT. Funny you should ask.

(She takes the torn up check from the coffee table and holds it up for DAD to see.)

DAD. *(Sees the torn up check)* What's that?

KAT. The check you gave him.

DAD. Oh, I knew he would tear that up.

KAT. So what was that all about?

DAD. Oh, I couldn't let Kevin loan Brittney the money. So I gave him the check, he gave it back and I slipped it back in his pocket when he wasn't looking.

KAT. And the ten thousand more if he changed my mind about Somalia?

DAD. *(Laughs)* Are you kidding? That was a joke. No one can change your mind.

(TRISH and BRITTNEY come out of the kitchen.)

TRISH. Dinner's almost ready.

DAD. Great…oh, one thing first…earlier I made a proposal to Trish.

KAT. *(Looks up, to herself)* Mom, I need you.

DAD. Did you say something, Kat?

KAT. No, no, go ahead.

(**MOM** *enters from the hallway.*)

DAD. Okay, we have the green light from the girls, and I am awaiting the verdict from the proposee.

KAT. *(Looks at* **MOM***)* I'm sorry, I just have one question. I have to ask this... Trish, where were you on September 5th? The night of the accident?

DAD. What are you doing?

KAT. You need to see the light.

TRISH. I'm sorry, what are you asking?

KAT. I just have to know where you were that night, just to put any doubt to rest.

DAD. You don't have to answer her.

TRISH. You think I was the drunk driver?

DAD. She's had a traumatic event. She's not thinking straight. Please forgive her.

TRISH. No, that's okay. I need to tell you. I should have told you a long time ago.

DAD. Told me what?

TRISH. The night of the accident, I was at The Mayo Clinic.

DAD. *(To* **KAT***)* She wasn't here. She wasn't the driver that hit us.

TRISH. And I didn't go away after Peggy died.

DAD. I thought you said you went to Ohio. That's why you missed the funeral.

TRISH. I stayed in Minnesota. I'm sorry. I lied.

DAD. Why?

TRISH. I was sick.

DAD. What happened? Are you okay?

TRISH. I had a congenital heart defect.

DAD. *(Taken aback)* How extensive was it?

TRISH. It was serious, but I'm fine, now.

DAD. Well, that's good. That's the important thing. Did they put you on meds?

TRISH. No.

DAD. No?

TRISH. I had a heart transplant.

KAT. Whoa.

DAD. *(Stunned)* A heart transplant?

TRISH. Yes.

DAD. Why didn't you tell me?

TRISH. It was your wife's heart.

(**MOM** *gasps, putting her hand to her heart.*)

BRITTNEY. Oh, my gosh.

DAD. *(A beat)* I'm sorry, I thought you said you have my wife's heart.

TRISH. I do.

KAT. I didn't see that coming.

BRITTNEY. Me neither.

DAD. I… I don't understand.

TRISH. Peggy knew I was sick, and she offered to donate her heart to me. I thought they might have told you.

DAD. Well, I knew she donated her heart. I just didn't know who received it. I didn't wanna know.

TRISH. I'm so sorry I didn't tell you before.

DAD. How did I not figure that out?

KAT. You've never seen her scar.

BRITTNEY. Never?

(**KAT** *nods "no" to* **BRITT**)

DAD. Okay, I'm confused. Have you been nice to me because you feel sorry for me? Or is it because you feel guilty that you have my wife's heart?

TRISH. No. I fell in love with you.

DAD. Then why didn't you tell me until now?

TRISH. I don't know. I should have. I'm sorry. I'm a terrible person.

BRITTNEY. No, you're not.

KAT. *(To* **TRISH***)* Wait a minute, did you know that you and Mom were a heart donor match before taking the job?

TRISH. No, I didn't.

KAT. The odds of being a match are pretty remote, aren't they? What? One in a million?

TRISH. I guess I see it as a miracle.

KAT. "A miracle?"

BRITTNEY. It <u>was</u> a miracle.

TRISH. *(Emotional, to* **KAT***)* I don't know how else to explain it. I just know that your mother saved my life and there are no words that can express how thankful I am to her. I think about your mother every day and what she did for me and how I wouldn't be here right now without her. I have her heart and I can feel the love that she had for you and for your family, and she's gone and I can't even thank her for the gift that she gave me.

MOM. You just did.

DAD. I'm sorry, I can't do this.

TRISH. Do what?

DAD. *(Emotional)* I can't be with you knowing you have my wife's heart… Do you know how painful it's been to lose her? I'm the one who should have died, not her. A man should never have to watch his wife die. I should have gone first. And what's worse, it was my fault. We didn't have to go out that night. It was my idea. She didn't even wanna go… It was my fault that she died, and I have to live with that for the rest of my life… I can't do it. I can't be reminded of that every day.

TRISH. We can take it slow. Please. I don't wanna lose you.

DAD. You know, I think I just need to be alone for awhile. Maybe it's best if you leave.

TRISH. I'm sorry. I should have told you. I'm so sorry.

DAD. Please.

TRISH. Okay. You're right. I'll go…

(*She composes herself.*) I'll just get my things.

(**TRISH** *goes in the kitchen, followed by* **BRITTNEY**. **DAD** *goes in the den, leaving* **MOM** *and* **KAT** *in the living room.*)

KAT. So, you gave Trish your heart. And to think all she wanted was a "get well" card.

MOM. Yeah, that was no picnic. We did all the testing and paperwork, the living will, the matching. And yes, it was a miracle that we matched. And no, they do not make it easy to give someone your heart. Trust me, it's not for everyone.

KAT. Did you know she actually had the transplant?

MOM. No. I wasn't there for the transaction. They don't show you everything. I mean, I felt a little lighter, but…

KAT. (*Changing the subject, she holds up the journal.*) So, you couldn't have just said, "Hey, Kat, Dad went to your events. Read my journal."

MOM. You hated it when I gave you the answers, remember? You always told me you wanted to figure it out on your own.

KAT. Why does anyone listen to me?!

MOM. Why wouldn't I?

KAT. Everything is upside down.

MOM. Not everything. You asked about the logic of someone like me dying. What about cause and effect, good things come from bad. Trish gets a donor, Brittney gets a business, you're good with Dad, and I get to see you in a dress. Oh, and you solved your simultaneous equation.

KAT. Not quite. I didn't solve Kevin.

MOM. Well, you better get on it. Partial credit is…

MOM & KAT. …for weenies.

KAT. I know… So, what about you? Do you get your wings? I mean, you gave the gift of life to Trish. That's gotta count for something.

MOM. Oh, that was nothing.

(Emotional) My greatest gift is you, honey. I'm so proud of you and I love you so much and I wish I'd said that a lot more.

(**DAD** *enters from the hallway.*)

KAT. *(Emotional)* I love you, too, Mom. I just wish I could have helped you.

MOM. *(Looking at* **DAD***)* You <u>can</u> help me. I know what I have to do now.

DAD. *(To* **KAT***)* Who are you talking to?

KAT. *(Thinks)* Mom.

DAD. Your mom is gone. She's not coming back.

MOM. *(She steps toward* **DAD***, on his right.)* Honey, I'm right here.

DAD. She's not here.

KAT. Yes, she is.

MOM. Honey, it's me.

DAD. Stop it. That isn't funny.

KAT. *(Stepping toward* **MOM***, on her right)* Mom is here. She's standing right here.

(**KAT** *touches and holds* **MOM***'s right hand.*)

DAD. *(Looking at* **KAT***)* Your mom is not coming back!

MOM. *(Putting her left hand on* **DAD***'s right shoulder, still holding* **KAT***'s hand with her right hand.)* I'm right here, Jack. I'm right here.

DAD. Stop it!

KAT. I didn't say anything. You were looking at me. It was Mom.

(**MOM** *takes* **KAT***'s left hand and places it on* **DAD***'s right shoulder. During the next few lines,* **MOM** *moves around to* **DAD***'s left side, continuing to touch his shoulder with her right hand as she moves.* **KAT** *keeps her left hand on* **DAD***'s right shoulder. When she gets to* **DAD***'s left side,* **MOM** *then moves her hand down to* **DAD***'s left hand and holds it.)*

MOM. Honey, I don't have a lot of time.

DAD. "A lot of time," who said that?

KAT. It's Mom. She's here.

MOM. Honey, it wasn't your fault.

(DAD *looks at* KAT *who nods, "go ahead, talk to her."*)

DAD. *(Looking straight out)* I am so sorry.

MOM. *(Holding his left hand)* You have to stop blaming yourself.

DAD. I don't think I can do that.

MOM. Yes, you can. You're strong. Don't worry about me. I'll be fine.

DAD. I miss you so much.

MOM. I miss you, too. Listen, Trish is telling the truth. I offered her my heart. She didn't know we were a match. She didn't even want to accept it, but I insisted. Please give Trish a chance. She's a wonderful, loving person and you'll be good together. I mean, she may not have the wit and charm that I have…or the outrageous lovemaking skills–

KAT. Mom!

MOM. I was awesome in the sack.

DAD. She was an animal.

KAT. Dad, Mom, back on message!

MOM. I need to let you go. That's what I have to do. I've been holding on to you, and it's been unfair. I love you so much, but I have to let you go. You need to move on and live your own life.

DAD. No one will ever replace you.

MOM. I know. Just know that I'll always be with you, in here.

(She touches his heart with her hand)

DAD. Please don't go.

MOM. I have to, honey.

DAD. I love you so much.

MOM. I love you, too.

(MOM lets go of DAD's hand, kisses her hand and touches his cheek with the hand she kissed, then crosses around to KAT. DAD touches his face where MOM touched him, sensing her touch. He looks straight out, as if in a trance. MOM takes KAT's hand off DAD's shoulder and holds it.)

(To KAT, holding her hand) Take care of Dad, will you? He needs you.

KAT. *(She nods.)* I will.

MOM. Goodbye, sweetie.

KAT. Goodbye, Mom.

(MOM heads toward the hallway, turns back, gives KAT the "I love you" sign in sign language, then exits thru the hallway. KAT turns back to DAD.)

(She touches DAD's arm and he "snaps out of it")

She's gone.

DAD. What just happened?

KAT. Mom went "full ghost."

DAD. She what?

KAT. Mom was Patrick Swayze, and I was Whoopi Goldberg and you were Demi Moore. And Mom talked to you and then kissed you, and do you have any idea how much therapy this is gonna take?!

(TRISH comes out of the kitchen with her purse and tote bag, and starts walking toward the door. BRITTNEY enters standing by the kitchen door.)

DAD. Wait, Trish, don't go. Please.

(TRISH stops.) I was wrong. It was just too much for me to take. I didn't know how to…how to react. I'm sorry.

TRISH. It's okay. I understand.

DAD. I think maybe if we just take it slow, we can, I don't know, maybe we can work thru everything.

TRISH. What made you change your mind?

DAD. *(Looks at* KAT*)* I don't know, I guess I saw the light…

(To TRISH*)* So, what do you think? Can I have another chance?

TRISH. Of course. Everyone deserves a do-over.

DAD. Thanks.

(He kisses TRISH *then hugs her.)*

TRISH. I guess I'll go check on dinner.

(She goes in the kitchen, hugging BRITTNEY *as she passes her.* BRITTNEY *stays.)*

DAD. *(To* KAT*)* I'm gonna miss you while you're in Somalia.

*(*DAD *goes to the bar and takes a photo of* MOM *out of the drawer and sets it on top of the bar.)*

KAT. You know, I've been thinking about that. I have an operations manager that can oversee the installations. I can probably swing it so I'm only there for a week or so every month during the start-up phase.

DAD. That would be great.

KAT. You're gonna get sick of seeing me more.

DAD. Not a chance.

KAT. I love you, Daddy.

DAD. I love you, too, Princess.

*(*KAT *and* DAD *hug.)*

BRITTNEY. Group hug!

*(*BRITTNEY *joins in and hugs* DAD, *sandwiching him between herself and* KAT.*)*

*(*KEVIN *walks up.* BRITT *sees him out the window.)*

Oh, hey, Kevin's back. *(To* KAT*)* I called him and told him you wanted to apologize.

KAT. You what?

(Everyone looks out at KEVIN.*)*

KEVIN. *(Walking toward the door, looking back at* **MRS. NORQUIST***)* Yeah, I'd like to help you out there, Mrs. Norquist, but I don't think that's what they mean when they say, "stimulus package."

(He turns to the door.)

BRITTNEY. *(She opens the door.)* Come on in.

*(***KEVIN*** enters.)*

KEVIN. Vikings beat the Packers!

DAD. Now, <u>that's</u> a miracle.

KAT. You came back.

KEVIN. Yeah, I got this invitation to a birthday party and I hear there's free food.

KAT. So, you came back for the free food?

KEVIN. Yeah. Well, that and to ask you out, after the apology.

KAT. Wow, that's pretty direct.

KEVIN. Someone said the shortest distance between two points is a straight line–

*(***KAT*** quickly kisses him.)*

BRITTNEY. Oh, another do-over!

TRISH. *(Popping her head out of the kitchen door while holding a small dinner/butler bell)* Dinner is ready!

(She rings the dinner bell)

*(***KAT*** looks up to Heaven. ***TRISH*** continues to ring the bell. Everyone sees ***KAT*** look up, and they look up, too, to see what she's looking at, as the bell rings into the blackout.)*

(Blackout)

End of Play

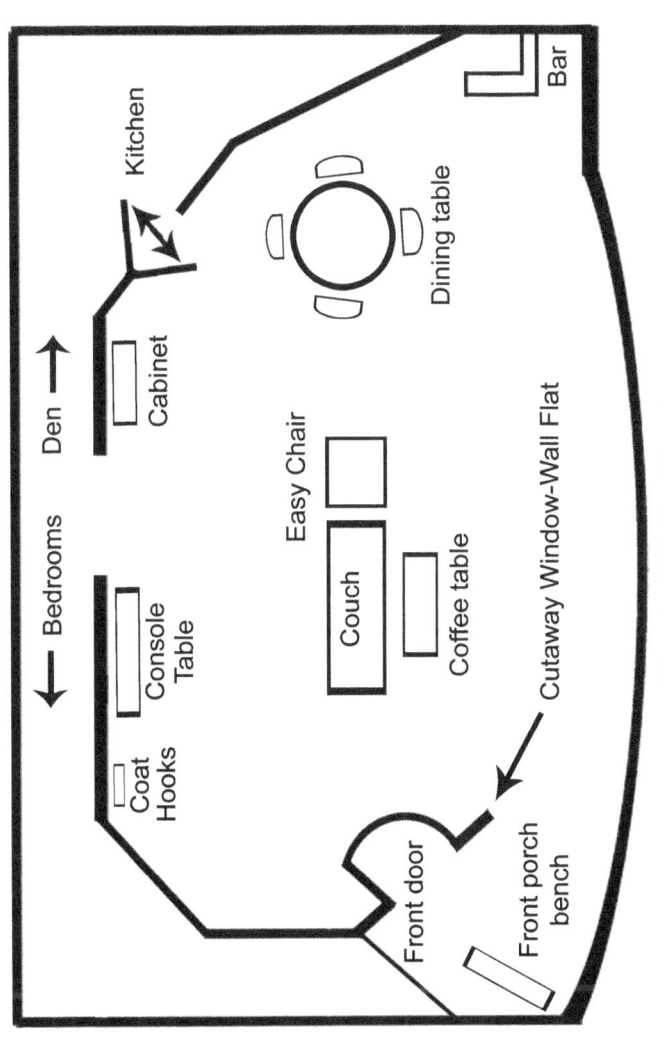

Mom's Gift Set Design
(For set photos visit MomsGiftThePlay.com)

Mom's Gift
Cutaway Window-Wall Flat

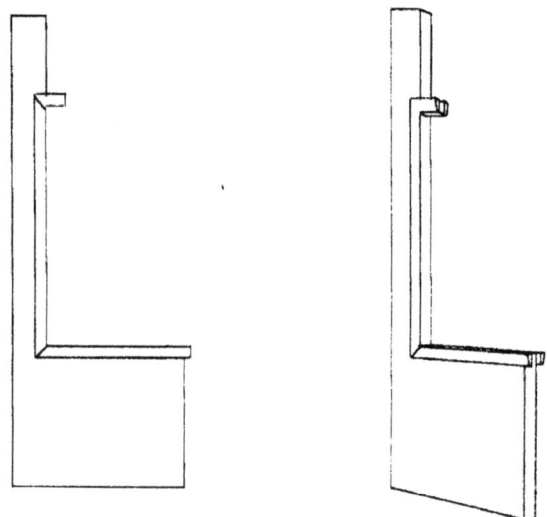

PROPERTIES LIST

ACT I

Onstage Furniture – 1 dinner table; 4 dinner table chairs; 1 bar with various liquor bottles on the bar; 1 coffee table; 1 sofa; 1 easy chair; 1 China cabinet; 1 console table; coat hooks on wall; 1 front porch bench

KAT brings in – Bottle of Cabernet wine; Laptop computer in a computer bag; Purse; Contract and pen in computer bag; Cell phone

TRISH brings in – 2 grocery bags; Purse; Tote bag

KEVIN brings in – Bottle of wine

DAD brings in – Bag of groceries

Other props – Cell phone (**BRITTNEY**); Purse (**BRITTNEY**); Tray of muffin tops (**BRITTNEY**); Wine glass (**BRITTNEY**); Plates/silverware/glasses (**BRITTNEY**); Bottles of beer (**DAD, KEVIN**); Bottle of Scotch (**KAT, DAD**); Bowl of Chips (**DAD**); Diet Coke (**DAD**); Car Keys (**DAD**); Scotch glass (**KAT**); Tray of appetizers (**TRISH**); Happy Birthday table centerpiece (**TRISH**)

ACT II

Glass of water (**KEVIN**); 2 suitcases (**KAT**); Business plan (**BRITTNEY**); Journal (**BRITTNEY**); 1 suitcase (**BRITTNEY**); Drivers License (**BRITTNEY**); Check (**DAD**); Photo of Mom (**DAD**); Small dinner/butler bell (**TRISH**)

COSTUME PLOT

KAT – Pants; Comfortable shoes; Sexy dress (Act II)

BRITTNEY – Bathrobe; Jeans/cute top; Nice dress (Act II)

MOM – Nice dress (maybe what she was buried in)

DAD – Sport Coat; Slacks

KEVIN – Sport coat; Slacks

TRISH – Conservative top with high neckline; Skirt